Strange Tales

Book One

Jason W. Bullard

Order this book online at www.trafford.com
or email orders@trafford.com

Most Trafford titles are also available at major online book retailers.

Print information available on the last page.

ISBN: 978-1-4907-5785-8 (sc)
ISBN: 978-1-4907-5784-1 (e)

Trafford rev. 03/25/2015

www.trafford.com

North America & international
toll-free: 1 888 232 4444 (USA & Canada)
fax: 812 355 4082

Contents

The Pet

It was a dark and stormy night. The creature moved swiftly through the woods, hoping it left everything behind in the lab. The creature didn't want to see humans again, if the creature would see any it would attack and kill them. The creature reached a small abandon cabin and crawled inside. Here it could finally rest and once feel safe again, the dark eyes of the creature slowly closed listening to the raindrops hitting the sinking roof.

A few miles away up a path from the cabin, through the woods was a beautiful house. The house was sky blue with white trim. It had a huge arch in front of the little sidewalk leading to the front door. A new family was going to move in the next day. Their last names were the Henderson's and they had a son named John. John was a 12 year old boy about 5 foot with dark hair. John had a female golden retriever named Lady, it was his first pet. She was a great dog and very smart, this helped out John when he had to train her. The family couldn't wait to move in to their house, they have waited a long time to buy a house, this was like their dream coming true for all of them. The family thought luck was finally on their side and yet did they know their lives would be changed forever.

The next morning the Henderson's was at their new house, just as the mover were already taking in their things in to the house. Mr. Henderson got out of the car first, walked over to the movers to make sure that they didn't break anything. John looked at his and shook his head, John's dad had to have everything perfect or close enough for him to be happy. Mrs. Henderson was totally different person and didn't harp on every little thing to be right. John got of the car with Lady. He stood in front of the house in awe, he knew that is parents had to pay a lot of money to buy this house. He remembered the heated discussion that his parents had a while back about the house and how much that it put them behind.

John walked in the house passed his dad who was directing the movers where to put everything. He walked up the stairs turn to the right and walked down the hall to his room. His room was located at the end of the hall and his bedroom window looked out over the front yard. He could see his mom standing by the car next to the movers truck. The house was far from town, John noticed the long dirt driveway from the house that led to the pave road which could take you to town. He all so noticed the house was covered by woods as far as he could see from his bedroom window.

The realtor Mr. Wakefield showed up just as the last of the items were moved inside the house, he stepped in the doorway and yelled hello. Mr. Henderson came to the door and shook Mr. Wakefield hand.

"So, I see everything's going pretty good Mr. Henderson. I just came by to go over the small details about your new house."

"First of all, call me Steve and let's go ahead and take care of those details."

Mr. Wakefield opened up his brief case that had the folder he needed for Mr. Henderson. He looked over the papers inside the folder to make sure he wasn't going to forget anything to tell him. "Well, it looks like you have to sign here and the only thing I have to tell you is that you own the woods around your house a few acres. There is a trail by the side of the house that will take you in the woods, you all so own a cabin that is in the woods too."

"All right, I think I got all of that where do I sign."

Mr. Wakefield showed him the line he was supposed to sign, handed him a pen and Mr. Henderson signed it. They both shook hands again and Mr. Wakefield put the papers back in the folder. He then place the folder back in his brief case and left the house.

John walked up to his dad as Mr. Wakefield was leaving, "What did he want dad?"

"He was just tell me that we own some of the woods and a cabin."

"That's cool, so can I go play in the woods to find the cabin."

"As long as you are careful. I believe the trail is over on the side of the house, it supposed to be a hiking trail."

"Okay, dad I will make sure that I am careful."

Steve Henderson went in to the house to see his wife Cindy. He thought that maybe she might have some idea for supper. He loved his wife very much and hoped that with this new house things would be better for them. The other house they lived in before was a leaking ship, he always fought with his wife about how much the repairs cost. They couldn't get ahead and nothing ever seemed to go their way. Their landlord was no help and when he put a bid on this house he couldn't believe it when they called him. Now since he sign the last of the paper work this dream home was now theirs.

John went to the side of the house and found the trail to the woods. The trail was wide enough for a few people to walk on it. The trail led off down a small hill in to the woods. He could see that when the trail disappeared in to the woods, it was a little darker and looked spooky. He looked at the sun that was all most setting for the day. He decided that it would be better for him to go tomorrow in fresh daylight. He could explore more and take Lady with him. He made his way back in to the house to see what his parents were doing.

"Hey, mom where are you."

"We are in the kitchen dear, deciding what to make for supper."

John walked in the kitchen and saw his mom at the stove. His dad was unpacking some more boxes putting the dishes away that he could find. John noticed that his dad was all so putting some can goods away in the pantry that was next to the refrigerator. John looked to his left and noticed the kitchen table and took a seat. He just sat when his mom said, "Well, supper won't be done for about 45 minutes. So go upstairs and put some of your bed together, instead of just sitting there."

John agreed and walked up to his room in a slow motion pace. The bed was already put up, so all he had to do was put his sheets and blankets on. His pillow was one of those long ones that would cover the length of the headboard. The pillow was green with a huge white S in the center of it. It was a gift from his grandmother who lived in Michigan. He hadn't seen her in a few months but she always seemed to write to him. He was lost in thought thinking about his grandmother when his bed was finally made, since he still had time he started to unpack some more boxes. He was on the last box when his mom yelled at him that supper was done.

John ran down the stairs as fast as his legs would let him. The smell of the food made his stomach growl and move. He didn't realizes how hungry he was until his stomach told him. He made his way to the dining room, where his mom had everything sitting on the dining room table. He could see mashed potatoes the real ones not the instant box ones, corn and the juices meat loaf he ever laid his eye's on. Supper lasted about an hour, John was taking his time and filling his belly. He thought he couldn't eat anymore, his mom brought in a homemade bake apple pie. He had a couple of pieces and felt over stuffed with all this delicious food. He was glad that it was Friday because he would have the whole weekend to play in the woods and do a lot of exploring. He all so needed a good night sleep.

The night brought a cool, nice breeze blowing through the woods. Cindy was standing on the back porch enjoying the weather. She never noticed that something on the out skirts of her eye site, hiding in the darkness watching her every move. The creature eyes were a dark color, its thick body hair was blowing in the wind and its razor sharp claws dug deeper in to the ground. The creature had special vision and could detect body heat, to the creature every human looked like the color red. This was great for the darkness because the creature could hunt at night without being detected. Cindy decided to take out the trash to the side of the house where the garage barrels were kept. She walked slowly and never noticed the creature getting closer to her. The creature was about to jump on her, Steve yelled from the back porch. Cindy hurried and tossed the garage bag at the barrels and ran to her husband. He opened up his arms and gave her a big hug. They both walked in shutting off the lights as they went.

The creature was furious and a low growl came from the creature. The creature went toward the garage bag sniff all around it. It smelled Cindy's meatloaf what was left and devoured it in a single bite. The creature loved raw meat but this would do for now. The creature went back in the woods to the cabin, the creature curled up in a ball and fell asleep. The creature dreamed of the lab, where they kept putting huge needles inside the cage, making the creature cry out in pain. The creature would get mad but the doctors would do this every day. The doctors were injecting the creature with different K9 DNA and alien DNA. The creature eye's started to change, its claws started to grow, it's started to get more hair, the creature grew in size, the teeth of the creature turn razor sharp, the hungry of the creature grew and so did the blood lust. The creature became super intelligent that it plan its own escape. All these memories came back to the creature, he showed its teeth and gave a loud growl.

Saturday morning was sunny and warm. John woke up, grabbed his everyday clothes, and headed downstairs for his breakfast. Mrs. Henderson had eggs, bacon, and toast on a plate for him. He was already devouring the food before he even sat down. The breakfast was good to his stomach and he even had a second helping. He was getting excited about going to explore the woods. Mr. Henderson told him that he needed to be home at least by supper time. He was smart enough to pack a lunch with him and he would for sure be in the woods most of the day. He hurried up with his lunch and ran toward the path, he decided to bring his dog Lady with him for companion.

The path was a dirt one with tall weeds up along both sides of it. When he stepped on the path and started walking, he noticed that the huge trees were keeping most of the sunlight out. Now the path was dark and mainly in the shadows compared when he first started in the morning light. He wasn't scared of the dark since he was six years old but the further he got the darkness consumed him more with a little fear creeping in to him. The woods was quiet and the only thing that he could hear was the sound of his feet crunching on some leaves on the path. He was glad he brought Lady her leash and he decided to put it on her so she would wander of the path. He didn't want to miss a single thing in the woods so he took his time. He thought he would hear more birds or some other animals but the woods remained quiet, he thought this was really strange. He wanted to make sure he could at least see the cabin that was the main goal for today's adventure. He just didn't tell his dad this because he didn't want to get in trouble. He walked a little further and noticed to his left a big grass clearing. He knew he was supposed to stay on the path but he wanted to play with Lady in the nice bright sun. He kept the leash on her because he didn't want to spend the rest of his day chasing after her and headed toward the clearing. It felt good to have the sun on his face and not be in darkness all the time. He played with Lady for about an hour and decided to head back to the path. He wanted to find the cabin so he picked up his pace a little. He didn't know of course that the creature was sleeping in the cabin avoiding the light because the sunlight hurt its eyes. The creature preferred the dark but if made to, could go out during the day.

Mr. Henderson was doing some yard work like planting flowers, picking up branches and just enjoying the day. Mr. Henderson saw the path as he was cleaning the yard, he got worried a little about his son but he knew he would be okay with Lady at his side. He looked up at the sky and he could tell that it was going to be a good day. He looked at his watch noticing it was two o'clock and decided to eat some lunch with his wife. He headed in the house and saw his beautiful wife cleaning the kitchen.

A car slowly was coming up their dirt driveway, until the car came in view of the house. The driver shook his head and hoped no one lived in the house. He exited his car and made his way to the front door. He noticed another car off to his right and knew for sure someone lived here and they could be in danger. He knocked on the front door.

Mr. Henderson just finished his lunch as he opened the door and saw a short man standing on his porch. The man said, "Hi, my name is Dr. Young. I was wondering if I could walk around your yard."

Mr. Henderson didn't understand and replied, "Why do you want to walk around my yard?"

"I will tell you in time, but I need to look around your yard first, ", said Dr. Young with a concern voice.

Mr. Henderson could see the concern look on the doctor's face. The two of them decided to go check the yard. As the two of them were searching the yard, they came across the garbage pails located by the side of the house. Mr. Henderson didn't get a chance to get to this side of the house, so he didn't know about them. The garbage pails were covered in some kind of slime and the doctor knew right away that it was the creature. The doctor was scanning the area and noticed a dirt path going tn to the woods.

"Mr. Henderson, did you noticed anything last night around this area?"

"I never saw anything. This is the first time today I been to this side of the house, what is going on?"

"Mr. Henderson, we need to talk right away this is very important. I will tell you everything."

Mr. Henderson thought it would be best if he sent his wife on errands, so she wouldn't freak out. He all so didn't want her to ask twenty questions about what was going on. Mrs. Henderson saw the doctor gave a smile and left to go do her errands. He watched his wife from the living room window get in the car and waited for the car to leave. He then asked the doctor to join him at the dinner room table.

The doctor sat and took a deep breath for he spoke. "I am going to tell you something that is unbelievable. I was doing research on an animal with a special K-9 gene that I found impressive.

"I don't understand what this as to do with my family."

"I am getting to that, see the animal became really smart and escaped."

Mr. Henderson was afraid to ask this question but he needed too. "Do you think this creature is here somewhere and getting in my trash."

"Yes I do, but I all so fear that your family is in danger. The creature is very dangerous and could kill you."

"You are sure that it will try to kill?"

"Yes the testing we did made the creature very anger and aggressive towards us."

"What do you mean us?"

"I had co-workers helping me with this research, they all ended up dead, the animal killed them."

All Mr. Henderson could think about was his son out in the woods with some animal that could kill him. Mr. Henderson stood up and in a loud voice said, "My son is in the woods we have to go get him now."

"Of course, we will go right away. So you know the creature is huge like a black bear and we should not to anger it in any way. The daylight will help but if the animal is in the woods the trees will make a nice shade for it."

"Let's go if there is anything else you need to tell me doctor, you can tell me on the way."

John was having the time of his life. He noticed the cabin in the distance and he got all excited. He started to run towards it and couldn't wait to explore it. As he got closer Lady stopped in her tracks. He pulled on her hard but she wouldn't budge, then his stomach started to growl. He decided it was time for lunch, so he found a log sat down and shared his lunch with Lady. Lady was restless and started to bark. The bark echoed through the woods and it woke up the creature. The creature let out a low growl and showed his teeth.

They ran outside and Mr. Henderson was leading them to the dirt path. He turned around and noticed that Dr. Young was not behind him. Dr. Young was by his car and in his glove box he kept his 9mm hand gun. He put it in his pants and caught up with Mr. Henderson by the dirt path. Mr. Henderson didn't; care what Dr. Young was doing and together they speed walked down the dirt path hoping they would find John.

John was all most out of breath by the time he reached the cabin. He sat on the broken steps to catch his breath. The cabin was falling apart but the main foundation was really good and he was shocked how well it looked. He walked up the steps to look in one of the windows to see what was inside the cabin. The inside was run down and the floor boards were all rotted. He decided to go inside and do some more exploring, when he walked the wood would make a creaking sound. He made to the front door and turned the handle. He pulled Lady along with him, she kept pulling back but he pulled her harder towards him. He opened the door and walked inside, Lady didn't want to go in but he made her. The door made a loud squeaking sound from the rusted door hinges and then the door fell to the wood floor. This made him jump back and Lady started to bark. He pulled on her leash to get her to stop.

The creature heard the noise and raised its head. The creature stood up and walked toward the sound. An anger raised inside the creature and a low growl a merge from its chest. The creature smelled the air and its teeth showed through. The creature started to drool and stretched its massive frame.

John thought he heard some noise and walked farther in the cabin. He notice a staircase and looked up the stairs to see if he could see anything. He now could hear movement because of the wooden floor boards. He noticed a doorway further down the hallway and saw red glowing eyes staring back at him. It took him a few minutes to realize that he was actually seeing this. A fear was creepy in him then he saw fangs, he couldn't see in great detail because the sunlight wasn't shinning in that room. He saw enough then he heard a deep growl. Lady started to growl and her hair was standing on end. He started to step back to get out of the cabin, it was the only thing he could think of doing. He reached the front door but saw that this creature was moving toward him, the creature was wide as the door way and its fur was pitch black. He turned to run and let go of Lady's leash by accident but he heard a big crash behind him as creature came for him. He started to cry as he was running, he couldn't help himself, he was so scared and thought he was going to die. He was running so fast he didn't see a root poking out of the ground, he tripped on it falling face first in to a tree. He picked himself up and turned around being face to face with the creature. He was sobbing so hard his chest was moving up and down in a fast motion. The creature raised his massive paw that had huge claws on it. He closed his eyes to prepare himself for the impact but Lady came to his rescue by biting the creature's leg. The creature's paw missed John and hit the tree right above his head. He opened his eyes and took off running before the creature could have another chance at him. He did turn around to see the creature take Lady in to the cabin. He was running so fast that he didn't realizes that he wasn't on the path anymore but running further in to the woods.

Mr. Henderson and Dr. Young were about to the cabin when they saw a tree that had a huge claw mark in it. This made Mr. Henderson really worried and he started to yell for his son. Dr. Young grabbed Mr. Henderson and covered up his mouth. Mr. Henderson got made and pushed the doctor off him.

"You don't understand Mr. Henderson, the creature could be close by."

"I don't care about that, I want my son and I will do anything I can to find him."

Mr. Henderson didn't even look at the cabin he was scanning the woods to see if he could see his son. He kept yelling for his son but there was no answer. He started to get upset and was totally scared about losing his son. He walked off the path and went deeper in the woods. Dr. Young stayed where he was and he decided to check out the cabin but thought better of it.

The woods kept getting darker, that is at least what John thought because he was so scared. He finally stopped running and sat on a log. He kept looking for his shoulder he was so sure the creature was running through the woods at him. He kept hearing branches breaking and trees moving. He thought for sure the creature would come out and grab him. He started to cry, he thought he would never see his parents again or his dog. He put his head in to his hands and continue to cry, there was a loud cracking sound he spun around to see his dad emerge from the trees.

"John, it is you. I heard you crying and I followed the sound."

Mr. Henderson picked up his son in a big hug not wanting to let him go. John was so excited that he hug his dad so hard and he didn't want to be let go. They were like this for a few minutes, then Mr. Henderson put his son down and led him back to the path. As they got back to the path they noticed Dr. Young coming towards them in a hurry.

"We need to leave now, I will get some more help to finish off this animal," said Dr. Young in a worried voice.

Mr. Henderson didn't argue and with his son hurried down the path. They kept quiet and made sure they were listening to the woods. They were half way to the house when the creature jumped out of the bushes at them. The doctor grabbed his handgun that was in the back of his pants. The doctor fired hitting the creature in the hind leg. The creature turned his attention on the doctor slowly walking towards him. The creature saw him early outside the cabin and the creature hated him. The creature lunged on the doctor before the doctor could get another shot off. The gun fell to the ground and the doctor fell on his back. The creature was in his face and the doctor had the creature by the throat.

John noticed the gun laying on the ground and he picked it up. He walked over to the creature, which still had the doctor pinned down. He pointed the gun at the creature and pulled the trigger, the motion from the blast knocked him down on his butt. Mr. Henderson picked up his son and they started to walk to the house again. The doctor waved them on, he decided to stay behind and to take another look at his creation.

As the doctor saw the son and father disappear around a bend, he decided that he would bury the creature. He didn't want anyone to know about his secret experiment and he hoped he could pay off the father. He didn't think anyone would believe them and he would make sure of that, he saw his gun on the ground and picked it up. He fired another round in to the head of the creature just to be sure.

Mr. Henderson and John heard the gun shot just as they saw their house. They were so happy to be home. They came in the back door near the kitchen and saw Mrs. Henderson making supper. She smiled at them and said, "Well it's about time you guys got home, I thought supper would be cold before you got a chance to eat it."

John spoke up first, "Well I lost track of time and dad came to get me."

"Okay, well that explains why Lady was here all by herself without you."

John looked at his dad with concern and his dad looked the same way. The two of them went to go find Lady. John went to the front door and went outside to the porch, he yelled for Lady and all he heard was a voice that sounded to him like the doctor. He closed the door and then he heard a low growl. He turned around to see Lady on the stairs staring at him, her eyes were glowing bright red and her teeth were showing. He never seen her this way before, he couldn't cry out and he was frozen in fear.

To Be Continue............

The House

The house was huge, gloomy and dark. The house sits in the country about ten miles from town. John Stone saw the house listed in a real estate magazine, it caught his eye and he was real interested in to looking at it. His girlfriend Kathy Glass was thinking about moving in with him, so she came up with this idea about a bed and breakfast inn. He liked the idea and figured that they would be partners and he all so wanted to marry Kathy since he laid eyes on her. He was taking his time in asking her because she was married before, it was a abusive marriage and it hurt her physically, plus emotionally. She finally got the courage to leave him before she ended up dead. She then met John, who made her happy and safe. They have been together for two years and he thought this house would be a great start for them. It didn't take long for him to get the house and he was all excited. He was leaving a week early to get going on their bed and breakfast idea. Kathy wanted to work a little longer before she had to quit, so a week was fine with her. He asked her to marry him before he left and she was so happy she said yes. He hugged her tight in his arms and couldn't wait for their bed and breakfast inn to be a success.

Day One

John left the next morning to the new house, he took some supplies with him like food, water and paper goods. He took enough of his clothes until Kathy could come up to join him, the bigger stuff would be moved later on. The house was a two hour drive, so most of the scenery was farm lands, he didn't mind because it was a nice beautiful day and the sky was blue. He never seen such a beautiful site since he was a kid, his parents always dragged him every summer to some cross country trip. As an adult now he could see the beauty in the great outdoors.

The house came in to view, he turned on to a long driveway that led up to the house. On both sides of the dirt driveway were big open fields as far as the eye could see. As he got closer to the house he noticed that the dirt driveway circled in front of the house, this would help his guest drop off their luggage before they would park their cars. He decided that he was going to do that now and then head in to town before he got late. He parked in front of the main doors, got out of his car and unlocked the house doors. As he opened the doors he heard the door make this awful creaking sound. The sounded sent chills down his back, he hurried up and loaded all his things just inside the house in the front hallway. He would explore later when he came back from town, he locked the house doors, got his car and headed for town.

John stopped by a small grocery store and walked inside. He saw a clerk when he walked in by the cash resistor. He decided it would be nice to go introduce himself so he went to the clerk, "Hi, my name is John Stone, I just bought a house on the out skirts of town."

"Well, hello I am glad to meet you. My name is Joe Bates."

"Hey, would you mind if I put up flyers for the bed and breakfast inn that my girlfriend and I are going to open?"

"I don't mind if you do. There is a board over there by the coolers that people put things on that they want to sale. Where is this bed and breakfast inn going to be?"

"I bought the house out by old miller road. It will be a few months for I get everything operational."

Joe gave John a strange look and in a low voice he said, "I wish you luck."

Joe then went to go do something to make it look like he was busy. John noticed how weird Joe got but didn't let it get to him. He picked up a few things like milk, eggs, butter and some juice. Apple juice was his favorite, Kathy thought it was weird to have with breakfast instead of orange juice. John paid for his items and realized he was a little hungry. He walked out to his vehicle and saw a restaurant. He went to the restaurant to get a bite to eat. He didn't take long to eat and was heading back to the house. The weather was perfect, he couldn't ask for a better day. He rolled down the window on his vehicle and let the cool breeze blow on his face. He drove up the driveway with happy thoughts, when he noticed a dark figure in an upstairs window. He got mad because he couldn't believe someone already broke in to his place. He drove right to the front door like he did earlier, slammed on the brakes, jumped out of the vehicle and ran to the front door. He made his way upstairs and was yelling that he was going to hurt the person who broke in to his house. He made it to the bedroom that he thought was the one, he opened the door and no one was there to greet him. He spent next few hours searching the whole house and he didn't find anybody. He sat down and took a few deep breathes, he figured it was his imagination and stress.

The day dragged on, John spent it cleaning the whole house. He had to keep his mind busy, he looked at his watch and realized it was time to eat. He then remembered he left all his items in the vehicle. He went back out to the vehicle and grabbed his groceries. He was mad at himself for being so work up that he would forget something like his groceries. He made his way to the kitchen and cook himself a meal, he wished he bought some bread, he would have to make another trip tomorrow to get his bread. The food helped him feel better and he went back to cleaning. He called the power and the water companies the day before so he was thankful he had some electricity. The day was about over and the sun was setting. He turned on some of the lights to help him clean. He felt dirty so he figured he would take a shower, he found his towel and decided to use the first floor bathroom. This bathroom was the cleanest, he would work on the second and third floor bathroom tomorrow. He all so had to check out the attic to see how it looked.

John left the bathroom door a jar when he got in the shower. A shadow walked by the door. He made sure the shower curtain was closed all the way, so he never saw the shadow. He was washing his hair but he kept getting this feeling that someone was watching him. He hurried up and pulled the curtain back to see an empty bathroom. He had a cold chill run down his back even thou his water was running hot. He decided that his shower was over and got out. He got his pajamas on then went to the living room, some of the furniture was left at the house so he was happy he something to sit on. He brought a scary novel with him and decided to sit on the couch that was left behind. He was getting to the novel but his eyes were dropping. The book fell to his chest and his head fell to the left. The house was quiet since he was the only one there but he could hear this ringing sound in his ear. The sound was getting louder and he opened his eyes to see a little girl looking back at him. He shot up looked around but the room was empty. He was glad he woke up because he left the lamp on but he didn't want to wake up scared. He giggled to himself, shut off the lamp and laid back down, drifting off to sleep.

Day Two

John woke up to the sound of knocking on the front door. He was moving real slow and sat up. He didn't know what time it was, the knocking was continuing and to John it seemed it was getting louder. He finally stood up and made his way to the door, he looked through the peep hole and saw a guy standing there that he didn't know. \

He opened the door and said, "May I help you?"

The man gave a smiled and said, "Hi, my name is Dean Reynolds. I use to know the family that lived here before you."

"Oh you did, that's great to know," said John in a curious voice.

"Yea, they were the Reins. They had two children a good family. There were here then one day they were just gone. The house sat empty for a long time before the bank took over and decided to sell the house."

John didn't know what to say at first the man just gave him chills. He put on a fake smile and said, "Well that is a shame because this is a nice house. I do have some things to do today, is there anything else I can do for you?"

"I am sorry, I heard in town that you are going to open a bed and breakfast inn. I was wondering if you needed some help I am looking for work."

"You know that isn't a bad idea, wait until my partner gets here and I will discuss it with her. If you leave your number and name I will call to let you know."

"All right, that is no problem. Thank you for your time and here you go this is my number."

Dean walked away to his car that was parked out front. He turned to give John a wave before he got in to the car. John returned the wave and watched Dean's car go all the way down the driveway. He closed the front door and went to go make breakfast, after breakfast he decided it was time to get cleaning. This time he started on the third floor, it took him along time to show signs that he actually had something cleaned. There was so much dust that he had to wipe more than once. The day was turning hot so he decided to open a few windows in some of the bedrooms to air out the place. He was hoping that it might cool off a little too. He stretched his arms above his head and decided to go check out the attic. He made his way to the attic door, he opened the door and made his way up the stair case. He looked the around the attic and realized that it wasn't that bad like the other floors. He was about to leave when he heard his name being whispered.

"Hello, is someone there?" John then laughed to himself, was he expecting for someone to answer him.

There was silence then there was a soft banging sounded echoing throughout the house. John was straining his hearing to see if he could hear where it was coming from. He left the attic and could still hear it. He knew the noise was coming down the stairs, so he made his way down and realizes that it was the front door. He was hoping it wasn't Dean again because he didn't want to talk to him again. He walked as fast as he could down the stairs to get to the first floor. The house was big and he was hoping that the person at the front door wouldn't beat the door off before he got there. When he finally reached the front door he looked through the peep hole. There was someone different at the door and he opened it.

"Hi, may I help you, ", said John.

"Hello there, my name is Sheriff Cliff Lawson."

"Hi, my name is John Stone. How are you doing today Sheriff?"

"I am doing good. I am going to ask you a question, did a Dean Reynolds come by here to see you?"

"Yes, he did this morning, is there a problem Sheriff?"

"There really isn't a problem but I would stay away from him. He was the last person to see the Reins family alive that is the family who lived here before you"

"Yea I know that, he said he was a family friend."

"He might have been but he was accused at the time for murdering them. He didn't get charged because I didn't have enough proof to keep him. I wanted to warn you and I will keep in touch with you. If you any problems with him or need anything just call me," the Sheriff handed his card to John.

The Sheriff left and John had a cold shiver run down his back. He went to the kitchen to get some water. He drank his glass of water and wondered why a man accused of murder would come back to the scene of the crime. He sat his glass down on the counter and decided to get back to work. He made his way to the front hall to where the stair case was located at. He climbed the stairs having his face looking down but he had this feeling something was watching him. He looked up to see a young boy looking down at him. This scared him and he lost his balance hitting his head on the banister knocking him out cold at the bottom of the stairs.

Day Three

John opened his eyes very slowly and grabbed his head. On the back of his head there was a huge bump. He got up, walked to the bathroom that was closest to him which was the downstairs bathroom. He turned on the water and opened the medicine cabinet to find some pain reliever. He shut the medicine cabinet, in the mirror he saw a man standing behind him. He hurried up and turned around and no one was there. He took another look in the mirror but only saw his reflection this time. He made his way to the living room, he sat on the couch and looked at his watch. He saw that it was already five o'clock in the morning the next day. He was out for about twelve hours, he took a deep breath and leaned back. He felt that he was losing his mind, he was alone in a big house, he knew he was a little stress but to see ghost. He laughed to himself and figured it was all in his head. He headed up stairs to sleep in one of the beds that was left behind. He figured he needed a nap before he got his day started. He found a bed on the second floor at the first bedroom he checked. He fell on it and went right to sleep.

John finally awoke it was already in the mid-afternoon, he slowly came to his feet and went to the bathroom that was right down the hall. He splashed some cold water on his face to wake himself up, he looked at the water in the palms of his hand and thought it was blood. He screamed stepping back away from the sink. He looked at his hands and brushed at his face to see if he had blood on him. There was nothing but water and he fell to the floor weeping to himself.

"What is wrong with me?" screamed John to himself with tears streaming down his face.

John then started to talk to himself which is something he never done. He wanted to talk to his girlfriend so he headed downstairs to the living room. He left his bag in the living room and it had his cell phone in it. He dialed Kathy's number, he rang about five times then went to voice mail. He waited a few then tried again this time it sounded like someone picked up, he waited for Kathy to say hello but there was just silence. He was about to talk when he heard an eerie voice talk to him, "Help us, you can't leave." He dropped the phone, his complexion turned paste white. He walked away from the cell phone to the front door, he had to get out, he tried the front door but it wouldn't budge no matter how hard he pulled on it. He was about to head to the back door when the cell phone started to ring. He walked over to it.

He picked it up and said, "Hello".

"Hello, honey how are you? Sorry I missed your call."

"I am doing… okay. When are you coming here?"

"It is going to be a few more days. I got some more stuff to do before I can leave."

"All right if you're sure. I just really miss you but I understand you have to finish your job."

"I am so happy that you are so understanding. I am lucky to have you, I love you and will talk to you later, bye."

"I love you too, bye."\

He hanged up the phone and cried silently to himself for a few minutes. He knew Kathy wouldn't understand what he was going through, so he decided not to tell her but he had to do something so he wouldn't go insane. He walked around the living room for a few minutes then headed out to the front hall. He saw a closet and decided to search it to see what was inside. He opened the closest and noticed a TV. He figured it must have been left behind by the Reins. He took it back to the living room to plug it in, the TV slowly came on and the picture was a fuzzy. He played with the picture, it came in better and he could tell it was some kind of western movie. The movie was already started so it was hard for him to understand what was going on but he made the best of it. He laid on the couch and started to drift off to sleep. He was about to sleep when he heard a loud thump, he sat up but was too afraid to leave the couch. He decided it could wait until tomorrow, he laid back down and was thinking happy thoughts. He didn't hear any other sounds except for the TV and went to sleep.

Day Four

The morning sun was bright and it shined right in to the living room. John slowly opened his eyes, stretched his arms above his head. He sat up and made himself get up to get dress. He decided today he would go outside to do some yard work and enjoy the fresh air. He headed out the back door which was located in the kitchen. He walked in the back yard and immediately knew what he wanted to do. He was going to sat up tables and chairs, that way his guests could eat outside to enjoy the warm weather. He noticed another back door further down from the kitchen one. He figured his guests could use that one to come outside why he used the other one to the kitchen to bring in all his supplies. He started to feel good about this and a smile came across his face. He saw a tool shed on the side of the house and went to go see what was inside it. The shed door made a creaking sound from the rusty hinges. He saw a push mower and some gardening tools. He looked at the grass and realizes that it needed it be mowed. He just hoped that he could get the mower running. He pulled the mower out of the shed and started to check all the fluids, the fluids looked good to him, so he crossed his fingers and gave a good hard pull on the cord of the mower. The mower didn't start the first time but after the fifth time the mower came to life. He mowed the back yard first then mowed the front. It took him longer then he thought it would and by the time he was done it was already in the afternoon. He was wiping sweat off his forehead, he felt dirty, hot and sticky from head to toe. He thought it would be a good idea to go take a cool shower.

John walked in to the house and realizes how much cooler it was compared to the outside. He decided to use the downstairs bathroom because most of his clothes were still in the living room. He grabbed some clothes and headed to the bathroom. The cool water felt so good on his warm body, he was about to turned off the water when he heard the bathroom door slammed shut. He jumped and moved the shower curtain as fast he could to see that the bathroom was empty. He hurried to shut off the water and slowly stepped out of the tub but some water leaked on the floor. His foot stepped on the water and he started to slip, he lost his balance and fell, hitting his head on the cold tile floor. He grabbed the sink to help himself back up and looked in the mirror, he noticed that his forehead was bleeding, some blood was dripping in to the sink. He grabbed a hand towel to try to get the bleeding to stop. The water turned on in the tub, he slowly turned toward the tub and a cold chill ran down his spine. He stood there for several minutes willing for his body to go shut off the water. He took one step forward realizing the tub was filling with water, he moved quicker this time slowly

The Sheriff saw John pointing down the hall, the Sheriff went down the hall and found the bathroom. John went in to the living room to wait, he was hoping the Sheriff wouldn't see anything. John kept playing with his hands rubbing them together really hard trying to calm himself. He heard the bathroom door open and footsteps coming toward him.

The Sheriff saw John sitting in the living room then spoke, "I empty the tub for you it was pretty full. You had a wash cloth stuck in the drain, I am surprise you didn't see it."

John put on a fake smile, "Well thank you, I must have dropped it and just didn't see it. You said you had some questions for me?"

"Yes I do, I was wondering if that Mr. Reynolds came back or if you found anything strange when you been cleaning the house?"

"No, he didn't came back. I don't know what you mean by anything strange?"

"Well, let me tell you this son. You looked pretty scared when you opened the front door. I find your tub full of water and all so when I said the word strange you got this weird expression on your face."

"If I tell you Sheriff you must not think I am crazy. I haven't been sleeping well and I think this place is haunted."

The Sheriff rubbed his chin, "Well, you are all alone in this house and I am not surprise that you are seeing things. I have some sleeping pills with me and they work really good."

The Sheriff handed the sleep pills to John. John took them, he figured if he did get a good night sleep that things would look better in the morning. The Sheriff let himself out, John didn't even move from the couch until he was for sure that the Sheriff was gone. He went in to the kitchen grabbed himself a glass of water taking the sleeping pills. He walked to the couch and laid down. He went right to sleep and didn't hear the voices who tried to wake him up.

Day Five

John woke again with the sunlight shining on his face coming in to the living room window. He tried to sit up but his muscles were all sore, he laid there moaning to himself but then his stomach started to growl. He had to get up to get something to eat before he got sick all over the floor. He slowly got up and moved toward the kitchen walking like he was some eighty year old man. Those sleeping pills he took knocked him out cold but he didn't feel any better, now he had a stomach ache from the pills. He looked at his watched and realizes that it was late in the afternoon. He decided to eat a hamburger with some chips, he knew why his stomach hurt so bad it was because he hasn't eaten all day. It didn't take long for him to devour his hamburger and he was right he started to feel better. He had a tall glass of water and saw a stool that sat next to a window, he decided to sit down on it. The stool was about four feet tall and made of wood. He slowly sat on it to make sure it didn't break under his weight. The stool held him and he looked out the window which showed the backyard. He could see birds flying around, making noise as they flew from tree to tree.

John was lost in thought and was wondering if the Sheriff was coming back to talk to him. He knew telling the Sheriff about the house being haunted was not a good idea. He knew he was right but if he couldn't tell his girlfriend why would he tell the Sheriff. He shook his head and put a hand on his forehead. He looked up again to the window and it was now dark, he stood right up looking at his watch. He couldn't believe he sat here all day but he knew it was only in the afternoon, now it was nine at night. He felt that he was losing his mind because he lost like six hours. He walked back to the living room like in a daze and sat on the couch. He decided to turn on the TV to take his mind off what just happen. The TV came on and the picture came in clearer, the weather was on saying that tomorrow was going to be hot with rain in the forecast. John laughed to himself thinking that he would be hot, sticky and wet trying to clean his house. He laid down to watch the TV but it didn't last long, he fell asleep.

Day Six

John woke up this time to a banging sound, he sat up to hear where it was coming from, he thought someone was knocking on a door. He got up and slowly started to walk, he thought it was coming from the kitchen. When he got to the kitchen the first door he saw was the basement door. He tried to open it but I wouldn't come open. He never went in to the basement since he has been at the house and he really didn't know why he never checked it out. He kept standing in front of the basement door lost in thought when thought he heard something in the dining room. He went to the dining room to look around, he happen to glance out the front window and saw the Sheriff's car out in his driveway. He hurried to the front door so he could met him to see what he wanted. He opened the front door but the Sheriff was not standing there, it was Dean Reynolds.

"You scared me, I was about to knock," said Dean with a little stutter in his voice.

"Hey did you see the Sheriff out there any where?"

"No, I saw his car that's right over there but I assumed he was already in the house with you."

"Speaking of cars, where is your car at Dean?"

"Oh, I had some trouble up the road with my car. I figured I was close to your house so I walked here to see if could use your phone to call for road service. I would all so like a drink if you got one, it is really hot out here today."

"Yea, sure that is no problem. Come in and I will get you something to drink while you use the phone."

John let in Dean and took another look around the front yard to see if he could see the Sheriff. The front yard was empty and the air was still, he looked up in the sky and could see dark clouds coming in. It was going to rain for sure today, it was a good thing Dean didn't get caught in a rain storm. He shut the front door and had Dean follow him to the kitchen to get him a drink. John got him a cold glass of water and handed it to him.

"Thank you. This taste really good and helps me cool down from this heat."

"You are welcome. Well since you are here I do want to ask you about the people that lived here. I know this going to sound crazy but I need to know. Did they ever say they saw ghost or thought this place was haunted?"

"I don't believe so, I mean they never said anything to me about any ghosts. Where did you say your phone was so I could call for help?"

"I will go get it, sorry if am freaking you out."

"It's okay, I know that you are here all by yourself and strange things happen when you let your mind wander."

John walked to the living room to where his cell phone sat on a side table next to the couch. Dean was walking with John right behind him, John picked up his cell phone handed it to Dean. John walked to the front hall by the front door to give Dean some privacy. What John didn't see was Dean took out the battery to his cell phone, then pretend to talk on the cell phone and hanged up. Dean then put the cell phone back on the side table and walked to where John was standing. Dean put a fake smile on his face as he looked right in John's face.

"Well I am waiting, why don't you tell me about the accident in the bathroom yesterday." asked Dean.

John thought about it and realize that he never mentioned that story to Dean. The only person he told was the Sheriff. He doubted the Sheriff would tell anyone since he really didn't believe him. He tried to smile at Dean to make it look like he wasn't terrified of him. There was so many bad ideas going through his head and the one that he stopped on was that Dean did something to the Sheriff.

"I, don't quite remember what happen," said John with a frighten voice.

"Oh, is that so, I just thought that I could help you since I use to know the family that lived here."

John just shook his head and knew he had to get away from Dean, "I am going to make some hot water for tea. I will be back okay."

"All right, I will wait here for you," said Dean with a big smile.

John turned toward the living room first to grab his cell phone before he headed in to the kitchen. He grabbed his tea kettle filled it with water and placed it on the stove. He turned on the stove and looked behind him to make sure he was alone. He tried several times to turn on his cell phone but the picture remain dark. He opened the back and saw the battery was gone. He took a deep breath, he needed to calm himself and had to get out of the house. He saw the back door and slowly tipped toe out the door. He waited a few minutes to make sure Dean didn't hear the door. He started to walk around the side of the house and loud thunder boomed in the sky. He looked up, at the same time he jumped. He grabbed his chest to slow down his breathing. He didn't hear Dean walk up behind him. John was about to turned but got hit in the head knocking him out cold. All John could see was bright light then everything went dark.

John came was coming around, he could hear a loud scream going off inside his head. He opened to eyes to see his arms tied to a chair, he looked around and realize he was in the dining room. The screaming sound was still going off but it was the tea kettle. He tried to push on the chair and rock himself, it was no good because he couldn't move no matter what he tried. He heard the tea kettle stop making noise and then footsteps were approaching him. He turned his head toward the doorway and in walked Dean with a cup of tea in his hand.

"I was wondering when you would wake up. I heard the tea kettle so I thought, why not go and make yourself a cup of tea," said Dean with a big smile on his face.

"Why are you doing this to me?"

"Well, it is a long story but I know you are trying to find out why the family went missing. You tried to make a run for it and I stopped you. I all so know that you been talking to the Sheriff."

"I really don't know what you are talking about, I am trying to start a business."

"Don't lie to me. I know you told the Sheriff about seeing ghosts. You just asked me today if I knew if the Reins saw anything weird here."

"I thinks it is all in my head. I just been a lone to much I don't know what I am saying anymore. I just want to live my life and forget this whole thing, it's been just a big misunderstanding."

"Why do you keep lying to me?" Dean was so mad he threw the hot cup of tea he was carrying in to John's face.

John screamed so loud that if he had neighbors they would have heard him. The tea was so extremely hot that his skin started to form blisters. He started to cry from the pain, to him it felt like his skin was peeling off. He lowered his head hoping the pain would go away soon. Dean just stood there staring at him with this mean look on his face, the tea cup still in his hand.

"I will get rid of you just like I got rid of everyone else. Now I have to move the Sheriff's car so don't you go anywhere," said Dean with laughter in his voice.

John had nothing to say to Dean, he was in pain and wanted Dean just to leave the house. He tried to keep his eyes opened but they were sore, the hot tea made blisters appear on his eye lids. He was listening to see if he could hear the door, he wanted to escape. The door slammed shut and John started to rock himself back and forth. The chair fell to the ground and it broke under his weight. He noticed that the rope was lose enough for him to use his teeth to untie himself from the rest of the chair. He slowly got to his feet and made his way to the back door through the kitchen. He was about to the kitchen back door, when he saw Dean through a window coming towards him from outside. He looked around to find a place to hide and the first door he saw was the basement door.

Dean entered the back door, he looked around the kitchen saw his tea cup sitting where he left before he went outside. He walked to the dining room and saw the broken chair and no John. He dropped his tea cup to the floor which shattered, he started to panic at first but angry over came him. He became furious and ran to the front door whipping it open, he looked around the front yard and up the driveway. He didn't see any sign of John, he decided that there was no way he left the house in time. He locked the front door and then he went and lock the back door in the kitchen too.

In a deep voice Dean yelled, "Where are you John?"

John was trying to find his way in the dark basement, he could hear Dean upstairs slamming doors and yelling. He didn't know where the light was because he never been down here before, he had his hands in the air looking for the string that usually is hooked the light bulb. He was trying to be quiet, his eyes were getting adjusted to the darkness and he had his back against the wall. He was taking baby steps but his foot hit something all most tripping him. He reached down to see what he all most fell over, his hands came across some clothing then he felt like a belt. He grabbed an item and realizes it was a flashlight. He turned on the flashlight and aimed at what was right below his feet. It was the Sheriff, his throat was cut. John took a deep breath to calm himself. John looked for the Sheriff's gun but it was not there, he looked around the basement with the flashlight to find a way out. He wanted to escape and fear started to creep in on him. He knew now if he didn't escape Dean for sure would kill him just like he did the Sheriff. He noticed a door in the back of the basement and headed toward it. He shinned the flashlight once more around the basement to see if there was another door, there was no other door so he was hoping the door he was looking at was his way out.

The door slowly creaked open and he stepped inside, the room was small and rectangular, he shined the flashlight around and found the light switch. He turned on the light which he had to shield his eyes from because it was so bright. He shut the flashlight off and put it in his back pocket. He kept putting his hand up to his face his eye's still hurt from the hot tea earlier. He didn't see a door in the room but he did notice that one of the walls was not cement like the other ones, instead it had wooden panels on it like it was covering something up. He went to that wall and started to pull on the wooden panel, it gave way with a huge crash and he was surrounded in dust. When the dust cleared he saw four bodies behind the panel, he felt sick to his stomach. The bodies were mainly skeleton but some still had hair on them. He just realizes that he made a lot of noise and he knew Dean would know where he was at for sure, he hurried to shut off the light and the door. He needed a place to hide just in case, he turned the flashlight back on to look around. On the floor he noticed a cell phone lying on the floor. He picked it up and turned it on. He saw the screen come to life and for the first time he knew there was hope.

Dean was making his way through the house when he heard a crashing sound in the distances. He stopped to listen closely to see what the direction the noise came from, it then dawned on him where John could be at. He hurried to the basement door, he opened the door and turned on the light. He knew where the light was since he has been in the basement before, he saw the Sheriff laying at the bottom of the stairs. He slowly descended the stairs taking his time, he was trying to listen to see if he could hear anything. He reached the Sheriff at the bottom of the stairs and when he took a closer look he noticed the flashlight was missing from his belt. He hurried to the door in the back of the basement, he opened it turned on the light and saw that the wooden panel was gone. The four bodies were looking straight at him and he slammed the door shut.

"I know you are down here John. You need to come out now," yelled Dean so loud you could hear the rage in his voice.

There was no response only silence came back to Dean. He was hoping no one would ever find those bodies but of course someone did now he would have to kill John. He would make it look like John killed the Sheriff and he committed suicide. He knew there were only two ways out of the basement, the stairs that led up to the kitchen and the door that was located behind the bodies that led to the outside. He slowly walked around the basement to see if he could see any sign of John. He was about to give up when he saw this tall wardrobe and the door was partly opened.

"Well, you might as well just come out of that wardrobe since I know that is where you are hiding."

John slowly opened the wardrobe and stepped out. He kept his distance from Dean because he knew how dangerous he could be and he wanted to keep him talking so he said, "I was trying to escape but when I saw those bodies I knew you had to pay."

"Oh, I see you want to be some kind of hero and save the day." There was a short pause and he started again, "I couldn't control myself I liked Mrs. Reins, she wasn't having an affair with me but I did fall in love with her when I use to work for them as their gardener. I did tell her how I felt and she just threw my emotions back in my face and tossed me to the curb like a piece of trash. I lost control and well you know what happen next." Dean pulled a hand gun out pointing it at John.

"So, you thought you could get away with the perfect crime."

"Well, I would have if you didn't talk to the Sheriff or find the bodies." Dean then noticed there was a cell phone in John's hand and started to laugh. "Who are going to call on that cell phone since it don't work?"

"This cell phone, well it does work since I believe this belong to the Sheriff. I all so called the police which by the way, are still on the line listening to your confession about the murders."

Dean just looked at him with his mouth hanging opened. He hated to be in embarrassed and would have great pleasure shooting John. He was about to pull the trigger when he heard loud noises behind him, he turned around to see where it was coming from, the door where the bodies were hidden started to open. The dead bodies stood in the doorway looking at Dean, he started to shoot at them yelling at the same time. John took this opportunity to escape Dean and ran up the basement stairs shutting the door behind him. He ran as fast as he could to the front door trying to whip it open but it took him a few times before he realizes it was locked. He unlocked it then went to stand on the porch never looking back. The police just arrived as he got outside, he was so happy to see them. He bent over putting his hands on his knees crying softly to himself.

A police officer went to John to try to get some information about what happen and where the intruder was at. John tried the best he could, all he kept saying was basement over and over. The police officer signaled for the other officers to search the house and the basement. The officer that was with John made him sit down on the porch steps, John realizes that the storm was over and the sun was about to set. He never thought he would see the sun set again or see his girlfriend. He asked the officer for a phone and he called his girlfriend and told her everything.

A short time later John saw the police officers come out of the house and asked him, "Did you find Dean?"

"Yes, we did he was on the basement stairs. His face was pale white and he had a look of fear on his face. He was still holding the gun with such a grip it took three of us to get it out of his hands. You wouldn't know what happen to him would you?"

"No officer, I really don't. I had a chance to escape and I took it. I never looked back to see anything."

"All right, we will take you to the station until your girlfriend can come pick you up. It will be a few days before you can come back to your house, so we can do are investigation."

John didn't know what to say, so he just shook his head. The officer led him to one of the cars and put him in the back. He went to the police station and waited in one of their rooms for a few hours before his girlfriend showed up. She had tears in her eyes and hugged him real hard. He was so happy to see her and gave her a long kiss. He already gave his statement to the police earlier, of course he left out about the ghost and the dead bodies. He told his girlfriend not to say anything when he talk to her on the phone earlier. They walked together to her car and went to a motel that was located in town. John had a hard time to fall asleep, he kept tossing and turning. He looked at his girlfriend and she was already asleep. He got up, walked to the window opening the curtain and decided to look out. He noticed that a little girl was standing in the parking lot looking at him. He recognized the girl from the house, it was the ghost that haunted him to help her family. He had a cold chill down his back, he shut the curtain and decided he needed some sleep. He sat on the bed, took a deep breath and knew that tomorrow his life would be better. He laid down, closed his eyes and dreamed of his bed and breakfast inn.

Stuck in the Middle

Josh Lockwood was a great son and student. The thought of being smart all the time bothered him. He wanted to be the cool kid, the rebel, and the one that the girls notice. At age sixteen, five foot seven, and about 175 pounds. He wasn't a bad looking kid, short sandy brown hair, blue eyes, and he had a nice tan. He would go to the tanner twice a week. He didn't matter what he did, his brain always in the way. He tried to fail but it wasn't in his nature. The more he tried to get notice the more it didn't work.

There was about a month left of high school and Josh was determined to be notice. He wondered what he could do first just to get some gossip going around. An idea then came to him. He could target the star of the football team. It would have to be something that would at least give him star quality. He had to be sure that he wouldn't get caught. He would take credit for it when everything was all said and done. He had a plan and he knew what he was going to do.

The locker room smelled of old sweat and dirty feet. You could still faintly smell the scent of soup coming from the showers. Zach Long came out of the showers with a towel wrapped around his waist. His short dark hair was all most dry. All the girls thought he was hot with dark brown eyes. His features were smooth and he had a build of a god.

It was the long hours he spent in the gym working on his muscles. He walked to his locker and open it up. A big explosion went off right in front of him. It took him a few minutes to understand what happen.

Zach started to look at himself, and realizes he was covered in brown goop. He started to freak out, the smell of the brown goop made him gag, and he was for sure it was poop. He backed up a few steps, then ran back toward the showers. He didn't realizes how wet his feet were. He slipped and smashed his head on the hard cement floor. The smacking sound of his head echoed throughout the backed room. A small puddle of blood was under his head. His eyes were rolled back into his head. To him the pain was only a second long before he went into total darkness.

A few hours later, his parent's got worried and called around. No one had seen Zach and his parent's worried even more. They called the police but Zach had to be missing for a whole day before they could do anything. Mr. Long was furious and wanted things done now. He wasn't a patience man. He was yelling in the phone as his wife, a few feet away, was crying into her hands. Mr. Long had enough of this and hung up the phone.

The next morning as the janitor open the front doors to the high school, he went about his day cleaning. He made his way to the boy's locker room, when he saw Zach on the floor. The janitor stood frozen for a few seconds, before he got on the phone to call the ambulance. The ambulance didn't take long to get to the high school.

The news about Zach spread fast. Zach was in a coma. That day high school was closed due to the accident. The only clue the police had was the brown goop all over the locker room. The police knew that it was a joke gone too far. The only answer they needed now is who.

A sign was posted at the high school the following day. Everyone in the high school was in mourning. Josh however was freaking out and didn't know what to do. Josh had to think of anyone who might have saw him that day going into the boy's locker room. He tried to stay calm but it was hard. He felt guilty and besides that he thought everyone was watching him.

Josh turned a corner and was all most to his locker when Dan Henderson came up to him and said. "Hey, Josh what were you doing here yesterday?"

Josh turned real pale and his body temperature rose. He stared right into Dans eye's and came up with a lie. "I forgot something in my locker and came back to get it." Josh was hoping this lie would work.

"Oh, I see, I was just wondering if you saw anything. I thought you might be able to help the police."

"I didn't see anything. If I did I would have called the police." Josh was hoping that Dan would see how rude he was being toward him. He just wanted Dan to leave because now he didn't know what he was going to do. Dan looked at Josh as if he got his feelings hurt. Dan only stayed for a few seconds more then he left. Josh had to think of a plan of what to do next.

The rest of the school day for Josh was terrible and meaningless. He had Dan on his mind all day and couldn't think of anything else. He knew being only sixteen that the police might not throw the book at him. The problem was he didn't want to go to the police. He had to do something with Dan and scaring him was out of the question. He would have to take more serious approach. He was afraid how far he would go.

Later that night, Dan was walking home from the movie theater. The sky was dark, causing a gloomy setting.

A cool breezes was coming from the north. Dan had his hands in his front pockets and his head down. The wind was coming straight at him. He wished now that he brought a hooded jacket. He picked up his pace a little bit more. He thought that it might rain. He hated getting wet, a noise made him turned around but he didn't see anything. He got a chill that ran down his spine. He hated the feeling about being scared. He knew he should overcome it.

Dan's dad always said that he should be braver. Dan didn't like his dad all that much. He was lost in thought and never heard the footsteps approach him at a fast pace. By the time Dan heard the footsteps and turned around, Josh was standing right behind him. Dan was about to say something but Josh shoved a blade into his stomach. Blood poured over Josh's hand and it felt warm to him despite the cold night air. Josh saw Dan's eye's in a state of shock. Dan's lips trembled and he fell to the sidewalk. The blade ripping from his stomach as he fell.

To Josh's surprise he had no remorse over what he just did. He thought maybe he would shed a tear but nothing came from his eyes. Instead he felt relief and a calm came over him. He thought this was a weird feeling but he didn't let it bother him. He looked around to see if anyone, he started to walk home. He knew for sure that he would get away with everything. He had no more worries, he started to skip and hum to himself.

In the darkness Dan's younger brother was hiding in a bush just a little farther up the sidewalk, he wanted to scare his brother before they got home. He kept a hand over his mouth, so Josh wouldn't hear him. Carl Henderson knew Josh since he could remember and Josh use to hang out with Dan. Carl couldn't believe his own eyes, when he saw the scene in front of him. He had tears in his eyes and his stomach really hurt. He was afraid to move because he didn't want to die. His house was a couple blocks away. He didn't know if he was fast enough to make it. He waited for a very long time before he headed home.

Josh was safely in his bedroom, when Carl made it home. Josh was sitting on his bed, reading a book. He was so excited that he couldn't consternate on the book. He decided that he would stretch and do some exercises. He figured that way he would be tired enough to fall asleep.

Josh was just about done, when he heard sirens. He just brushed it off and didn't think they were for him. He walked over to his bedroom window to take a look. The realization that the police was in his driveway took him a few minutes to register. He started to panic and didn't know what he was going to do. On instinct he grabbed the knife off his dresser. He looked at the blade and there was still blood stains on it. He knew that his life was over. He decided that prison wasn't for him, so he would let the police take him out. He walked slowly down the stairs to the front door. His parents were all ready by the front door. Mr. Lockwood saw the blade in his son's hand. He tried to grab the knife from him but Josh pulled away. Josh then pushed his father down.

"It is my fault that they are here. I killed Dan and all most killed Zach." Josh was screaming at the top of his lungs.

Mr. Lockwood just stared at his son like he never knew him. Josh could see the disappointment on his father's face. He knew for sure that his father would never feel the same way about him. Josh opened the front door and ran at the police with the knife raised high. There was a lot of gun fire and by the time the smoke cleared, Josh lay dead on the sidewalk in front of his house by the porch.

The next morning the local newspaper had the story about what happen. The Lockwood's left town and would never return. Their son was buried in the local cemetery in a corner lot all to himself. Josh might have had his fifteen minutes of fame but even in death he was still alone. There would be no one who would visit his grave. He would be known as a killer and would never be the cool kid like he wanted.

The Mist

The night was cold. John was walking home from work at a fast pace. The wind blowing strong, he pulled up his collar of his black windbreaker. In the mist, he saw a woman getting attacked in the distance. He stopped in his tracks to make sure he was seeing the right thing. He couldn't believe what he was really seeing. The street lights didn't give off much light. He went to the lady and saw the man close up who was attacking her. The man turned and looked at John. His eyes were a ghostly green. He looked supernatural and inhuman. He told John "your next."

John was scared, he started to advance on them thinking that he could distract the guy long enough for the girl to escape. The lady was already dead from the huge blade that the man stuck into her gut. Blood spilled out on the sidewalk and ran along the sidewalk. He fumbled for his cell phone which fell from his hands on to the sidewalk. He turned and ran in the direction of his house with the killer slowly approaching him. John dug into his front pocket of his jeans for his keys. He saw a house with the lights on and ran to the front door. John knocked as hard as he could, but no one answered the door. John turned around and could still see the killer coming for him. He started to run further down the block. His house was only a few blocks away, so he could call the police from there. John made it to his house. He fumbled again with his keys, but finally got the front door opened.

He quickly slammed the door and locked it. He looked out the side window next to the front door to see if the man was there. By the stairs, he approached the table with the telephone on it. He dialed 911 and waited for someone to help him.

"Hello, 911 what is your emergency and how may I help you?" asked a woman's voice.

"I need help, there is some crazy killer after me and I think he followed me home." John waited for a response from the lady on the other end, but instead all he got was silence.

He panicked and slammed down the receiver. He heard a voice talking to him from the other side of the front door. "The police can't help you now. I will find a way in to kill you."

John ran upstairs to his bedroom and slammed the door locking it behind him. He heard a noise and he really didn't want to come out of his room. He had to check to see what was going on. He looked down the stairs and saw the man coming through the front door. All that John could see were those green eyes glowing in the dark, staring at him through the dim light of his house. He knew that this person wasn't normal and fear had a hold of him.

The killer said, "I will be up there shortly, don't go anywhere."

"Go away, leave me alone the police will be here soon."

The killer started to laugh and replied, "We will see if they make it before I cut your throat wide open."

John ran back towards his bedroom and locked the door. He was still looking for some kind of weapon to defend himself. He noticed this newspaper sitting on the night table. He moved it to see if he had his letter opener but he noticed the headline. His eyes got big and he held the paper closer to get a better look. The headline read "KILLER ON THE LOOSE." John didn't have time to read the article. The door started to fall in and John knew he had to do something. The killer started to laugh at him and told him that he was going to kill him. John looked around to see if he could escape. He opened his bedroom window and jumped out. The killer followed him. John looked towards the park that is down his street to see if someone could help him. Of course there was no one around. The killer started to get closer and closer. To John, it felt like the killer was almost touching his clothing. John saw a other house with lights on, so he ran up to the door and started to knock and he realize that it was the same house he was at before. No one came to the door just like before. He started to get upset. The killer was getting closer every time he stopped. John saw the carnival ahead of him, he forgot that they came to town this week. He climbed over the fence and he ran towards a pay phone to call the police again

"Hello police headquarters."

"Yeah, my name is John Lockhart and I am in real danger. A killer is after me, help me please!"

"Ok, sir, we will send a patrol car over right away. Where is your location?"

The killer jumped by the pay phone scaring John and making him drop the receiver. John ran further into the carnival hoping to find security offices. He was thinking that someone had to be on duty protecting the grounds. He was hoping this since he really couldn't think clearly. He had sweat pouring down his forehead and his legs felt like rubber bands.

The killer was getting close, "Death will come to you if I catch you." he laughed

John wanted to do was escape this nightmare. The killer pulled out a big knife from his belt. The killer knew where John was going he could read John's mind. John was getting tired and wanted to make a run. The killer made it to the offices before John could. John didn't know what to do, so he looked around and found a trash can. He picked it up and hit the killer right in the head, knocking him down to the ground. John looked at the killer, scared out of his mind. John walked a few yards away, the killer rose up behind him and walked towards him. John felt a chill, he turned around and hit the killer, knocking him down again. John began to kick the killer in the stomach, just to make sure he was knocked out. All the angry came out of John and he could stop himself, blood was coming from the killer's mouth

John walked slowly now, because his foot hurt from jumping out his bedroom window. He really made it worst by kicking the killer. He was waiting for the cops to show up. The killer came too. He smiled at John, as he rose to a sitting position. John couldn't believe it he knew he hurt the killer. John made his way to the fences as the killer sat there laughing.

John came up to the fence, took a deep breath and started to climb. As he was climbing, the killer eyes opened. He ran towards the fence in the distance, hoping to catch his prey. The killer noticed John was only half way up the fence. He grabbed John's leg with his left hand and with his other hand he brought the knife up, cutting John's leg. John fell from the fence, landing hard on his backside. John tried to get up but his leg was really bad. He couldn't think the fall injured his head. John rolled away trying to put some distance between him and the killer. John started to run but he couldn't. He needed to find a place to hide or defend himself.

John saw a house of mirrors and thought he could hide in there and maybe lose the killer in the mirrors. John kept hitting the mirrors hurting his head. This was harder than he thought. He thought if he stayed here long enough maybe help would arrive for him and he needed it. He heard laughter so he left through the exit door that was located in the back. He knew that if the killer was behind him in the house of mirrors that maybe he would have a chance to survivor. The mist was covering the ground now. This is where the killer love to murder his victims. His powers came from the mist and the blood that he drain from his victims. He didn't know the killer was never in the house of mirrors. John took a few steps away from the house of mirrors. The killer sneaked up behind him, stabbing him right in the back, pulling the knife straight up his back killing John. The killer heard a police officer in the distance approaching them.

"What happened here?" asked the police officer.

The killer said, "This crazy guy tried to kill me."

The officer looked at the dead body and turned to the killer. He was walking away and the officer yelled stop. The killer turned around lunging at him, slicing his throat in the process. The blood poured down the officer's shirt.

By the time the rest of the police arrived, the killer disappeared in the mist. The police couldn't understand why John went to the carnival to hide out. The police figured maybe he was so scared the he wasn't thinking straight. The case is still open and the police are still looking. They are all so hoping that this won't happen again.

Red Vine

The sun was high in the sky as Paul White made his way to Little Pall Hospital. His wife Jackie has been fighting cancer for years but this time it got the better of her. He had to rush her to the hospital in the middle of the night. He decided to leave early this morning to eat something and get some coffee. He drank the last of his coffee before he enters the hospital. He tosses the foam cup in a little waste basket by the door. He takes a deep breath before he gets to his wife's room. He love his wife very much but to see her in pain and all those wires hooked up to her, makes him shed a tear. He tries to hide them in front of her but she smiles a little. She tells him that it's all right. She then holds his hand but doesn't have the strength to squeezes. He led's in and kisses her on the forehead. She loves it when she feels his warm lips touch her.

He sits there in a uncomfortable chair all day, so he won't miss a thing. When he thinks that she is a sleep he will sneak out for a few minutes. He asked a nurse to get him a cup of coffee when nightfall comes. He is worried about her, this time the cancer has taken its toll. He can see that her skin is pale and to him it seems that she is getting weaker.

Her eyes flutter a little bit and he gets all excited. He speaks in a low voice just enough for her to hear him.

"Honey, can you hear me.

"Mum… yes." she says in a low voice all so but he barely heard her.

He leant forward a little more so he can hear her better. She is starting to wake up her eyes open but it takes a while. Her eye lids are heavy and with all her will power, it takes a toll on her.

"Oh, I am in so much pain. It feels like my insides are burning." she says why she makes a face that she is in agony.

He doesn't say anything. He nods his head in agreement. He is lost for words, he hates that his wife is going through this. They been married for only six years. In that time they have been inseparable. He grew so close to her that seeing her now in this much pain hurts him. He touches her face to try to make her feel at home. She gives him a little smile not much but enough to know that she cares.

She falls back to sleep with no problems. The pain killers has done its work again and now Paul feels lost. This time he knows that it's worse than before. He decides to go stretch his legs and clear his mind for a while. By now the hospital is dark and the street lights outside are dim casting him in shadows. He sees a bench and sits. The tears start to fall and he puts his head in his hands to drown out his sobs. He doesn't realize how long he sat until he hears the clock tower ring for one am. He jumps up and speed walks to his wives room. There is a night light on the far corner, so he can see without jumping into anything. The chair gives him no comfort. He manages so he can be close to his wife.

His dreams are bad. So, he tosses and turns all night having nightmares.

In his dreams he can't find his wife and he screams for her. He hears her voice faint. He tries to follow but a wall blocks his path. He pounds on the wall but he can't knock it down. He hears her scream louder now and he screams back. He awakes with his cheeks wet and his throat dry. He grabs his wives leg to make sure she is still there. He stands again to calm himself to keep telling himself that it was just a dream. He looks out the window to see the sun rising to start another day. He turned to see a nurse come in to check on his wife. All the vitals were fair but not good. Her heart was still weak and beating slow. He just nodded and grabbed his wives hand once again. She moaned in response but did not open her eyes. He knew right away that she was getting worse. His hands were tied and now it was up to God to help that is what he believed right now.

As the weeks went on she was just wasting away from his eyes. He kept his cool in front of her but late at night he would cry in the bathroom. He would bring her flowers that had red vines on them. She loved the flowers, she would smile every time. He would place them by the bed, so she could look at them all day long. He would sit there and talk to her even if she couldn't answer back. When she would show pain he would hug her, tell her now that everything would be alright.

One night as he was getting to sleep, he heard his wife whisper his name. He walked over to her to hear what she had to say.

"Paul… if I don't get better, please take my life I don't want to suffer anymore."

This put Paul in total shock and he took a step back. He just shook his head and kept saying no over and over. She just cried and shook her head yes. The pain was too great for her. After about five minutes of this, they just hug each other crying.

During the night Paul cried to himself and knew that he couldn't do that at least that is what he thought at the time. How could he take the life of the woman he loved? He sat there and the more he thought, the more he could do what his wife wanted him to do. His life would be nothing without her but to see her in so much pain hurt him too.

A few days later he found an old syringe that he would use. He found some medicine that he would use to eject into her IV. It would put her to sleep and pass away without any pain. Hopefully the doctors wouldn't realize that the medicine was missing until it was too late. His nerves were at their peak and he tried to remain calm. He felt that everyone was watching him waiting for him to mess up. He would wait until nightfall before he tried anything.

They talked and laughed for most of the day. She knew that it was the last day and she was prepared. He never said anything just laughed, he wanted to enjoy every minute with her. Sometimes the pain was so great that she would cry or shut her eyes. He would wait until passed and try to get her to smile. The day went to fast for him but he couldn't stop time. He stood by the window looking at the room. He stared at his hand and saw the syringe. He slowly walked to his wife's bed. He injected the medicine in the IV and said a silent pray. In the middle of his pray, the nurse walked in on him. He panicked and ran to the bathroom. He shut the door and locked it. He heard the nurse scream for help but he was too worried to figure out what he was going to do. He could hear people now hammering on the door. He looked in the mirror smashing it with his fist.

Now the bathroom door was hit even harder splitting the wood. Paul grabbed a large piece of glass shoving in to his throat. Blood spilling everywhere and he collapsed to the floor. As he hit the cold tile, the bathroom door busted open revealing nurses and security. In the distance he heard a doctor say, that he had his wife stable. A tear ran down his check and he felt his life slipping away. He closed his eyes seeing nothing but darkness.

The doctor tried to save him but it was too late. Jackie however survived about fifteen more days after her husband suicide. She finally took her own life. She wanted to be with her husband, her only true love.

"Sometimes love is blind and god is the only one who can take a life."

This is what it reads on their tombstone that is what Paul's brother, put on there to remember what happen that terrible day. He wanted to make sure that no one would ever forget and that he would know what is brother was really like.

Terror at Mills Creek

The night was cool and windy. Fall was in the air. Leaves were turning color and falling to the ground. The local park was quiet except for the merry-go-around moving due to the wind. It was like a ghost was pushing it and having fun at it. The merry-go-around was old and kept making this squeaking sound as it spun around. Maybe at late night ghost do play at the park, when no one is around. It is just weird how certain things move on their own at night, but during the day the playground equipment just stands still. Even if the wind is blowing really hard. From the merry-go-round down a hill, toward some woods was a creek. The creek ran right in front of the woods, there was a wooden foot bridge to get a cross to enter them. There lying face down at the edge of Mills Creek was a body. As cold as the night was, so was the body.

The small town of Milton was just raising up to the sun just coming up over the horizon. The people of the town was opening their business getting ready for people to come and shop. It was fall time, so the leaves were changing color and a cool breezes was sweeping through the town. All most everybody started their Christmas shopping early even though it was still about three months away.

Linda Baker was taking her morning jog through the park like she does every day. All that was on her mind was trying to think about what to buy her kids for Christmas because she knew if she didn't get it right away it could be gone. It drove her crazy that her son, and daughter could change their minds so fast when it came to buy them gifts. The jog itself was great, she felt really fit. She was thin, about five foot five, long brown hair and beautiful skin. She should have worn a hat because the morning air was a little bit chill. Linda always jogged by the creek to the main road when going through the park. When she was on the main road she would take it all the way home. Linda knew that if formed a big circle but she didn't mind, because if felt that she was on a big track.

Linda was half way down the side of the creek where the running trail went, when she notice something white up ahead. She was not a big girl but she could take care of herself if a problem would occur. The white image she saw was a shirt. When she got closer the whole picture started to come together like one big puzzle. She was staring at a dead body of a young teenage boy she thought. She turned around to see if she could see anyone around, she all so notice that the boy only had on his boxer's besides his shirt. She fumbled in her sweat pants to find her cell phone. She called the only person that could help her in this time of need.

Doug Baker was deep in sleep and having one of those good dreams. He kept hearing a ringing sound but in his dream he couldn't find out where it was coming from.

He realizes that it was a phone. He opened his eyes slowly and reached on the night stand for the phone.

"Hello, may I help you."

There was instantly crying and mumbling he could not make out. He repeated again what he said, then realizes that it was his wife on the other end.

"Slow down honey. What happen and where are you?"

"I… I am in the park by Mills Creek, where the foot bridge is at for the woods. I… I found a dead body."

Doug eyes were wide open now and he told her to stay where she was and he would be there shortly. He stood up put his pants on, grabbed his brown shirt and grabbed his gun belt too. He was about six foot, he had a built of a weight lifter, dark brown hair and hazel eyes. He was the sheriff of Milton and he couldn't believe that in a small town like this that a dead body would just come up out of nowhere. He grabbed his car keys off the key holder headed toward his car, started it up turned on the lights and drove like the devil toward the park where is wife was waiting for him.

Doug couldn't get the car to go fast enough to get to his wife. He drove the car off the main road right down the by the creek. In the distance he saw his wife standing there holding herself and shaking. He stopped the car and ran towards her. He pulled her towards him to give her a hug. He felt warm tears on her face soak right through his shirt. He hugged her even tighter to try to calm her down. He walked her to the car and sat her in the passenger seat. He then continue to walk towards the body but did not touch it. He knew that if he moved the body in anyway, that it might remove any evidence of who might have killed this person. The body lied on an angle and the skin looked like a deep purple. He figured it was the weather that change his skin color. He bend down to take a closer look and realize he knew who it was. By the angle of the body it looked like a person fell off the foot bridge and the killer set the body this way to pose it for anyone to see.

Doug walked back over to his car got on his CB and called for the coroners. He made another call to his deputy Todd Kincaid to come to the park by the creek because he found a body. Todd couldn't believe it either what he just heard. He told Doug he would be right there. Todd got off his personal CB and put it back on the hook. He saw that his hands were shaking really bad. He made a tight fist to stop the shaking but it only helped for a minute before he started shaking again. He put his mind on finding his coat and the keys. The morning sun was coming up slow but just high enough to shine in the sheriff station windows setting a large glare. He shielded his eyes, so he could make it to the car. The car started up with ease and he headed toward the park.

The park started to swarm with people, how they found out Doug couldn't figure out but he motion for them to keep back, so the corners truck could come to do their job.

The coroner's truck was a big blue moving van. The van had signs on each side stating that it was a corners vehicle from Milton Hospital. If some stranger didn't know better it looked like someone might be moving. The two men stepped out of the van and walked over to the body. The doctor his is Dr. Ronald Long was already examining the body. Doug called him right after he called his deputy. The doctor was an older man then Doug and lived in the town his whole life. He was the town doctor for these people. He was fifty years old, white hair showing on his black and about five foot six. As soon as he came on the scene he knew that the dead body was Chad Cross. Chad was a sixteen year old boy that was a sophomore in high school and on the football team. Dr. Ronald Long was Chad's doctor as far as he could remember. Dr. Long had a upset stomach seeing this kid lie here knowing that just last month he saw Chad for a physical, so he could play football. Dr. Long examine the body more closely and saw a six inch gape maybe about three inches long inside the boy's chest. A blow like that wouldn't have killed him instantly. The neck of Chad was all so broke, the doctor figured that after the blow the killer pushed him off the foot bridge which cause the neck to break. The fall like that which is about twelve feet would have killed him.

The doctor rose up and walked over to Doug and said. "Well, the corners can take the body now. I figured you are looking for a boot knife about three to four inches long that was attempted to piece the boy's heart."

"Ok doctor, what about the way the body is on an angle," said Doug.

"Well, that is because of the fall and all so when the killer removed his clothes the body shifted that way."

Doug shook his head in agreement and motion for the corner's to take the body. In the distances Todd was rolling up in his car right next to the corner's van. Todd jumped out of the car and walked over to Doug.

"Hi, Doug who was it that passed on."

"It… was Chad Cross. I need you to find his dad and tell him to head to the hospital to make a identification for sure."

Todd agreed and got back in his car. He knew that Chad's dad worked at the lumber yard. Ray Cross was his name and he was about six foot tall and weighed about two hundred and nine pounds. Ray all so was a drinker and could put away a lot of drinks. Ray's wife died a few years ago from cancer. It was that cancer that ate your insides away and before you knew it, you were already dead. Todd hoped that Ray wouldn't get hostile and threaten to kill everyone. The lumber yard was about ten miles from the park and Ray was known to start work early, so he could leave early. Ray loved the bar and would have a few before he would call it a night. He pulled the car in to the dirt drive that lead the way up to the huge metal barn. This is where they stored all the lumber for shipments or for the local community to buy. He pulled the car up to the office door. The office door was located on the front of a building, then the rest of the building was used as a warehouse. He took a deep breath and walked in the office. The office was a small room with a desk and a file cabinet. The floor had dark carpet on it and a smell like pine was in the air. There was another door of to his right that led to the warehouse, where the workers cut the lumber before they stored it in the metal barn. There was only one other chair of to one wall for customers to sit down.

"Well hi there deputy. What can I do you for this cold morning," said Gladys Ruin.

Gladys was the secretary for the lumber yard. She would answer the phones and right down orders. She would either give them to Ray, which he was the plant manager or to David Valley who is the owner of the lumber yard. David was well liked and everyone was shock that he put Ray as his second in charge. The community just figured that David could see something inside Ray that no one else saw.

"Hi there Gladys I need to talk to Ray Cross if you please," said Todd with a serious tone in is voice.

Gladys raised her eye brow in a curious matter and got on the phone to page him. He waited which felt like a life time for Ray to show up. He wanted to tell him the sad news so he could get it over with. Gladys kept her eye on Todd to see if he would advance on Ray, when he walked through the door. Gladys thought maybe Todd's intentions were serious and something must have happen really bad for him to be up here early in the morning. The door slowly open from the warehouse and a man stepped out.

"Well, Todd I guess you are looking for Ray but he called this morning. He said he would be running late," said David.

Todd looked at Gladys to see why she just didn't tell him that in the first place. Gladys said, "I didn't know that he called in David."

"It was real early before you arrived this morning."

"So did he say what time he would be in or where he was at," asked Todd.

"I assume he would be at home but he really never said what time he would be in Todd I am sorry I am not more help."

Todd shook David's hand and thanked him for his time. Todd walked out of the office and got back in his car. He headed toward Ray's house to see what was so important that he couldn't make it to work on time. Todd didn't drive real fast or out of control this time. He did the speed limit like he supposed to, so he would not draw any suspension to himself.

Todd made it to Ray's house that was run down. The paint was peeling and some of the trim around the windows was falling off. The porch had rickety steps and some steps had holes in them too. Even some of the upstairs windows had plastic on them to keep out the cold air. He made his way up the porch steps and watched for the holes, so he wouldn't not fall through them. He made it on the porch and went to the screen door. He open the screen door, which it needed a new screen because it was loosely hanging by a few threads. He knock on the door really hard and heard someone say to him hold on a minute. Todd did as exactly that because he definitely wasn't going anywhere. It took a few minutes for the door to open. Ray stood their pale white and looked like death warmed over.

"Hi Ray, I am Deputy Todd Kincaid may I come in?"

"Yeah, I remember you. I guess, I am supposed to get ready for work, but I feel awful. It is taking me a while to get around today."

Todd slowly walked through the door and first thing he notice was a tower of beer cans next to a arm chair in the living room of to his left. There was all so dirty dishes and filled ash trays all over the coffee table. In the air was a faint smell which to Todd smelled like a musty and stale smell.

"I guess you want to sit down right," said Ray in a rough voice.

"No, that is all right, I just have to talk to you I have some bad news. You might want to sit down."

Ray walked over to the arm chair and sat down. A look of disgust was on his face. Todd took a deep breath and looked at Ray, when he spoke to see his reaction.

"Well, this morning we found a body in the park by Mills Creek, which we believe might be your son. We need you to come to the hospital to make a positive id."

"This a joke right. I mean you are talking like this person is dead."

"Yes, this person is dead." Todd was having lumps in his throat when he talk, hoping that Ray wouldn't notice.

Ray just sat there and didn't shed one tear or even get mad. He spoke in a calm matter. "You can tell me, which son of mine it was right."

"I can tell you who we think it was, that would be your son Chad."

"I knew that son of mine shouldn't sneak out at night. He probable was up to no good, dam him."

Todd was shocked and didn't reply to his sudden out burst from him. Instead he just said, "I could take you up to the hospital and bring you back if that's what you want?"

"Yeah, let me call work to let them know that I won't be in for sure now. There goes a day's pay."

Ray got up slowly, made his way to the kitchen to grab his phone off the wall. Todd couldn't believe that even for him to be sick, that he didn't hurry up and get his stuff around faster. To him his instincts told him that Ray didn't care at all. Todd hoped that wasn't true.

"Before we leave I want to make sure that Chris got off to school," said Ray with a roll of his eye's.

Todd nodded and waited while Ray climbed the stairs to Chris's bedroom. He didn't have to wait long Ray came right back down the stairs walked to his coat rack and put on his coat. Todd led the way to his car, they both got in and it was one quiet ride all the way to the hospital. When they arrived at the hospital Todd asked if Chris was at school and Ray said yes. Ray got of the car without another word and walked to the hospital entrance.

Todd walked right behind him into the hospital and down the hallway to the elevator. The hospital had a bleach smell. It all so had a smell that you could never name, but you knew it was a medicine that the janitor's used. The elevator took the two of them down to the basement level. Todd as a kid never liked to come down here. The place gave him the creeps. The elevator doors open slowly and the two walk out and down the hall to the right was the morgue office.

Ray didn't even hesitate just kept on walking, that nothing in the world mattered to him. As he headed to the double doors, Doug appeared walking out of the double doors meeting the two of them. Doug nodded to Ray and he didn't not return the gesture. Ray just looked like he didn't want to be here.

"Well, Ray would you please step in here and we will take care of this as soon as possible," said Doug as nicely as he could.

Ray walked through the double doors where the office was, then straight back was another door. Behind those doors is where they kept all the bodies at. Ray waited for Doug and Todd to go first then he followed them through the other door. In the room, in the middle was a metal table and on the left was a wall full of draws. Ray walked over to the metal table the body was covered by a white cloth. The doctor that worked in the morgue was at the right wall working at his desk.

"Well doctor would you pull back the cloth please,' said Doug.

The doctor stood up walked over to the table and lifted the cloth back. Ray took a long look at the body, like he was in a daze. The doctor pulled the cloth back down.

"Yes, that is my son."

"I am really sorry," said Doug.

Todd looked real pale and put a hand to his mouth running from the room. Doug walked over to Ray and at the same time grabbed a clipboard off the doctor's desk. "I need you to sign this form to make it final," said Doug.

Ray looked at the paper grabbed a pen from Doug sign the paper. He then turned around and walked right back out the door without a word. Doug was a little concern that Ray didn't show any emotion over his son. Doug gave the doctor his copy of the paper and walked back out in the hall to see how Todd was doing.

"I guess you haven't seen that many dead bodies in your life," said Doug.

"I wasn't prepared for it. I guess it just put me in some kind of shock."

"Where did Ray go?" asked Doug.

"He went out to my car. I am going to take him back home. Doug, I have a strange feeling about Ray. Ray never once showed any kind of emotion, when I told him about his son."

"I noticed that too. I think we better just start investigating everyone that Chad knows starting with his brother."

"I know that Chris is at school. I all so know that he had a girlfriend named… Amy Lane."

"The major's daughter! That's just wonderful. Ok you question all the teenagers that he hung out with and I will see what Ray was up to last night," said Doug with his hands on his head like it was going to explode.

Todd agreed with that and walked to the elevator to go back to the first floor. He was glad that he was leaving the hospital. He just had chills all over his body. By the time that he walked out of the hospital, Ray was already sitting in the passenger seat looking straight ahead. He thought that Ray looked like one of those dummies that some women buy to make it look like they have a man with them. He walked around the car got in and started the engine up. The ride to Ray's house was about the same, when he took Ray to the hospital. He once again pulled into Ray's driveway. Ray got out without saying one word walked to his front door unlocked it and walked in with a hard shut of his door.

Todd glanced down at his watch and realizes he had some time before school had their lunch. He thought that would be the best time to go up to the school. He stopped down to a small coffee shop to grab a cup of coffee and a roll. He decided to sit down for a bit, maybe his stomach would stop twisting and turning. The sight of Chad's dead body lying on that metal table still gave him chills running down his back. He finish his roll left a tip on the table, grabbed his coffee and headed toward his car. The sun was a little higher in the sky and the chill of the morning was gone. He took a deep breath and took in the warmth of the sun, since he still felt cold from his head to his toes.

The drive to the high school was about forty five minutes from the coffee shop. Even a small town, Milton High School was pretty big. The grades were 9 through 12 and it was a two story building. The high school was on the out skirts of town so it could other kids from the nearby towns. The middle school was down the street but it was closer to town. The families that had a child in each school it was easy for them to transport their children.

Todd drove in the parking lot which was large and wide. He walked up the stairs to the front door. He made his way to the office which was on the left hand side as you entered the building. The secretary told him that Chris just went to lunch, so he would be in the cafeteria. He thanked her and headed that way. He walked by the gym and couldn't resist to look in. He opened the door and took a peek. He could smell body sweat of the people that were earlier. His memories came flooding back to him. He remembered playing basketball here and smelling that exact same smell. He missed those days boy did miss being the star on the court.

Todd realizing that he had more important things to take care of like a murder. He hurried a little faster to the cafeteria hoping to catch Chris in time. The lines to the cafeteria were long just like they were when Todd went to school. He made his way through the crowd and into the big cafeteria. There were round tables sat up with those plastic chairs about five to a table. This is where you notice the clicks that every teenager talks about. He notice Chris in the far corner sitting all by himself. Todd walked over to him and sat across from him.

"Hi Chris, how are you doing today."

Chris made a choking sound, it came from his throat then stuttered a statement. "I… am doing… just… I mean fine."

"Ok, Chris now I need you to come with me because I have some news for you."

"Could you just tell me right here or do I have… to go."

"I guess I could tell you here but it is not good news. I feel that it would be better if we were some where private."

Chris stood up left his tray of food and followed Todd of the cafeteria down the hall and into an empty classroom.

"Now, I want you to sit and listen."

Chris took a seat at the desk right across from Todd. Chris then looked right at Todd without even blinking.

"This morning we found your brother dead by Mills Creek."

Chris turn white and I mean so white that he looked like a clean sheet from the hospital. Chris started to cry and tears were flowing fast. Todd couldn't hurry fast enough for a tissue before Chris's cheeks were all wet.

"How… did he die?"

"Well, someone murdered him and we are trying to find that someone. Chris I need you to tell me besides his girlfriend, what other friends did he hangout with."

Chris thought real hard and then said. "He always talk to Dan Baker. I think they were best friends."

Todd was taken back by this because Dan was Doug's son. Dan was 16 years old, dark hair, about 6 foot, and weighed about 190 pounds. Dan sister which was his twin, her name was Sue. Sue had brown hair, about 5'5", and weighted about 120 pounds. Even thou they were twins, they didn't look alike. They always hangout with the same crowd and mainly were the same person.

"I guess that I will talk to Amy first, then I will talk to the Baker twins is there anyone else that you might have forgotten."

"I don't think so, I don't feel well and my chest hurts. May I go now?"

"Yeah go ahead and if you think of anything else please call us ok."

Chris agreed and left the classroom. Todd followed behind and made his way to the office, while Chris walked the opposite way. Todd talk to the principle about having the other kids coming to the office, so he could talk to them. He thought this would be better instead of trying to find each one of them. The principle agreed and said that he should have done that in the first place. Todd knew that there was bad blood between him and the principle ever since his freshmen year of high school.

Amy Lane was about 5'4", blue eyed blonde, and she was pretty thin. She wasn't thin like a skeleton. She was thin that looked good for her size. All the boys thought she was cute and Amy was however dating Chad ever since their freshman year, when he join the football team. Amy became a cheerleader and one day they started talking. They both hit it off together and ever since that day, they always were together no matter where the other one was going. It has been 2 years since that day. Todd knew that she would freak out and he would have to calm her down. Amy walked in the office and sat down at the nearest seat. Todd cleared his throat so that he could get it all out without stopping or pausing.

"Ok Amy, what I am about to tell you might be a shock. This morning we found your boyfriend Chad Cross dead by Mills Creek."

Amy eye's swelled up and the tears started to flow. She cried for several minutes before she responded to the deputy. "Are you really sure? I mean you know for sure that it was his body that you found."

"Yes, we made a positive I.D. of the body."

"I don't understand, when I saw him last night he was fine."

"About what time did you see him last night?"

"It was about 7 o'clock pm and he left about 8:30pm."

"Did anyone else see him leave about that time?"

"Yes, my dad did because he made the comment that it was getting late and Chad should go home."

"Ok so he was at your house. All right thank you for your help and if you happen to think of anything else, please let me know."

Amy got up but walked gingerly out of the office. She didn't realizes that her legs were all rubbery from the impact of the news she received. Todd could see that the news hurt her but he wondered could she just be a good actress. The next two teenagers he would talk to would be the Baker twins. Todd would talk to them together because they shared this close bond. He all so figured that if one didn't know the other one might.

Dan and Sue walked into the office real slowly. It was like they were in a different world here and didn't know how to act.

"Hello you two, why don't you have a sit right over there in those two chairs." He waited a few when they were seated he continued. "Now, I have some news that is not real good, we found Chad Cross's body today by Mills Creek."

The twins turn white and Dan was the first one to speak. "I just saw him yesterday, he left my house about 6:30pm and he said that he was headed to Amy's house."

"That does make sense since Amy said he arrived around 7." He mainly was talking to himself not the twins but they listen real closely to him.

Sue spoke next her quiet voice sounded shy. "I didn't know him as well as my brother did but he seemed ok yesterday, he seemed happy."

Dan said in a rush. "Besides that, he just caught a football scholarship this year. He was the youngest person to do so in this school."

Dan and Chad had played football together for years, so he knew that Dan wouldn't lie about this. They were best friends so they would share everything. Dan got real emotional and started to cry a little. Todd started to tear up and said. "It will be ok Dan. We will find out who killed him."

"You didn't say anything about murder," said Sue in a terrified voice.

"Well Sue, he was murdered and it wasn't pretty."

The twins sat there for a while before they could return to class. Todd kept telling them that it would be all right and their dad could fill them in on the rest. Todd then said bye, walking them to their class and he headed toward the front entrance. Todd made his way to his car, got in the front seat and took a deep breath. A tear came from his eye and a sadness filled him. He thought how could anyone be so cold to kill another human being?

Doug was headed toward the local bar called, To The Rim. Doug made it there just as Todd made it to his car to leave the high school. Doug waited outside the bar for about two hours before they opened. Doug was checking out the building and wondering if Ray himself would be heading down here. The bar itself wasn't that bad, it was real clean. The lighting wasn't the best. It was dark and gloomy. Doug made his way to the bar counter to the owner. The owner Stan Duke was a good man and brought a lot of business to the community. It was not just the bar but Stan did a lot of fund raisers throughout the summer months.

"Well what brings you here, I usually don't see you until New Year's Eve," said Stan.

"I am on police business Stan."

"Okay, so what can I do for you?"

"I need to know what time Ray Cross left this bar last night."

"I see… let me think it was around one am. I had to get a little mean with him, so he would leave that is how I remember the time."

Doug thought about it for a minute or so and then shook Stan's hand. Doug left the bar and headed toward the sheriff station to see if Todd had made it back. Doug was hoping that Todd would have some good information for him, so they could solve this case. Doug pulled in front of the sheriff station and notice that Todd was there, so he made his way in and saw Todd sitting at his desk all quiet. Doug walked over to Todd and sat across from him.

"I take it didn't go all that good at the high school?"

"I am… really not sure because everyone's story checked out," said Todd with sadness in his voice.

"Well, that means everyone told you exactly where they were at last night."

"I guess, wait a minute Chris never said where he was at last night. I just assumed he was at home."

"You didn't ask him for sure or question him," said Doug in a mean voice.

"I didn't, man I messed up. I did question the other kids like Amy, Sue and Dan."

"Sue and Dan my kids are involved with this too."

"Yes, Chad was at your house last night seeing Dan before he left and went to Amy's."

"Okay, so Chris Cross was the only one who didn't say where he was last night or should I say you didn't ask him," said Doug with a little laughter in his voice.

"I saw him break down in tears and I ask who his brother friends were and lost my train of thought."

"It's all right Todd we will give him until he is out of school and we will head to his house to talk to him."

"I all so think we better talk to the mayor," said Todd.

"Why."

"I think he saw Chad last night before he was murdered," said Todd in a choked whisper.

It was like clockwork no sooner, they were talking about the mayor when he walked in the sheriff's station. "Just the man, we wanted to see," said Doug.

"I know all about the matter, my daughter called me from school all upset."

"I guess you know that we have to ask you a few questions," said Doug.

The mayor agreed and had a seat. The mayor told them that he did send Chad home at 8:30 almost 9p.m. somewhere between then. He said that Amy went to bed shortly after that so did he. It hurt the mayor because he had high hopes for Chad. Chad would have put Milton on the map with his football skills and the scholarship to match. The mayor all so said that Chad seemed happy and was not worried about anything. The mayor just sat there for a few minutes lowering his head shaking it in sadness.

"I didn't mean for your daughter to get all upset. I just wanted to know all the facts," said Todd.

"I understand and I hope you capture this murder before he hurts anyone else," said the mayor as he stood up and stormed out of the sheriff's station.

Doug sat there looking at the mayor's fast exit before he turned to Todd. "I think from now on we will be talking to people together so there will be no more problems."

Todd agreed and the two of them hopped in the sheriff's car. They were headed to Chris's house to see where he was last night.

"I got to ask you one question?" said Todd.

"All right go ahead and ask me."

"When you were in New York City was it really bad for you with all the murders and violence going on?"

Doug thought for a minute before he answered, "It was really rough and when the mayor offered this job to me because he heard of my skills, I accepted with no regrets."

"I understand, I mean who would have thought in a small town there would be a murder?"

"You are right Todd, I thought I left that all behind me, when my family came here to live and leave New York City behind us."

There was silence for a while between the two of them. Todd didn't mean to stir up any old memories that would make Doug upset. Todd just felt that it must have taken a lot for a great detective like Doug Baker to pack all his things and bring his family to a small town like Milton. Todd glance at Doug for a while to see if he could see any signs of emotions coming from his face. There was none but determination showing to solve this case. Doug however was thinking about New York City, when he had to shoot that teenager or be shot himself. The teenager only had to be about sixteen years old. Doug did it in self-defense but the scar was too deep for him to stay any longer. That's when he applied for this job to be sheriff. Doug all so had to think of his children growing up in a environment that may cause them their lives. Doug couldn't even talk to a psychologist about the incident and always had nightmares. Doug never talked about it or thought about it much until now. Todd did stir up some memories but to Doug maybe it was time that they be brought up instead of being forgotten. Doug needed to be done with it and let his inner demons be lose. He did his job right and he should not feel guilty for what the outcome.

They approached Chris's house and pulled in the driveway. They both got out and walked up to the front door. It was just like before but this time they both had to be careful not fall through the porch. Doug knocked on the door pretty hard, there was no answer so he knocked again even harder. They both waited for a few more minutes, then when Doug was going to knock again he decided to push on the door and it slowly opened.

"Did you hit open?" asked Todd.

"I don't believe so, I know I pushed on it but not hard."

Doug pushed the door open a little more and slowly reaching for his gun. The door opened to reveal the contents with in. There was Ray Cross sitting in a wooden chair with a shot gun in his mouth. The shot gun already had been shot killing Ray instantly, his brains were all over the ceiling and scattered all over the wall. Doug still cautions walked slowly never taking his hand off his gun.

"If he didn't opened the door, then how did the door open," said Todd.

"I think I must have opened it, when I knocked the first time causing it to come lose from its hinges."

Todd walked on the other side of Doug and came around the left side of the chair Ray was seating on. Todd notice that Ray's left ankle was tied to the leg of the chair.

"Check this out, I think this is weird," said Todd.

Doug was going to take a look when they both heard a noise at the front door.

The door was not shut all the way there was a slight gap that you could see the outside. Doug motion for Todd to stand on the right side and Doug pushed opened the door. On the porch was a cat. The cat was sitting on a loose board which made a noise when the cat would move. Doug then moved toward the chair to see what Todd was talking about earlier. Todd pointed to Ray's left ankle. Doug kneeled down to examine the scene and noticed that the other ankle had some sticky residue left behind on this pant leg. Doug figured it had to be some kind of tape but he wondered why just tape the one leg. He realized why, it was because someone else taped his legs and tried to rip the tape off but they must have interrupted the killer. Now Doug had two murders on his hands and he had no idea who the killer was, he all so didn't want to deal with the mayor.

"Hey, Doug do you think that Ray knew the killer and was taken by surprise."

Doug turn toward Todd. "I believe your right on that and he didn't even have time to react."

The front door creek opened, Doug reached right for his gun pointing in the face of Chris Cross. Chris was scared and he started to turn white. He looked around Doug to see his father in a chair.

"What is going on here, dad… dad answer me."

Chris broke down, he started to cry and fall to his knees. Todd walked over to help him up and took him outside. Doug radio for a corner to come pick up the body.

Doug was going to get an autopsy done for sure on Ray, even thou there was no hard evidence he was darn sure he was murder. The coroner didn't take long to show up and Doug told him he needed that autopsy as soon as possible.

Doug decided he needed to go home it was getting late and he would call the mayor tomorrow to let him know what was going on. Todd told Doug that he would take Chris to his house and social services could be called tomorrow to see what they could do for him. Doug agreed and headed home to his family, he couldn't get the picture of Ray in the chair and he wondered why Ray. Doug knew that Ray didn't have a lot of money. Doug felt sorry for Ray but that wouldn't help him get any answers on this case.

Doug pulled in to his driveway slowly. He got out and made his way up to his front door. Doug gave a big sigh and opened the door. Linda Baker was waiting for her husband like she always did and gave him a big hug and kiss. Doug returned the hug and kiss back to his wife, then they went in to the dining room to get his supper which was reheated for him. This was the first time he missed supper with his family since they moved to his small town of Milton. Doug sat down said a prayer and started to eat, a few minutes later Sue came up to her dad, "Dad I really need to talk to you."

"Okay honey, what is so important that you couldn't wait until morning to tell me."

Sue looked at her feet and whispered a little in her response. "I should have told you as soon as I found out but I was scared for her."

"Who are you talking about?"

"It's Amy Lane and the night Chad Cross died."

Doug's attention was all on his daughter and the next sentence that would leave her lips.

Sue continued, "Well, you see they got in a fight and Chad slapped her so hard that she had a bloody nose."

"Why didn't she come forward and tell me?"

"She was afraid that you would think she killed him."

Doug stood up, walked over to his daughter and gave her a hug. Everything that Doug knew was nothing to teenage drama. Doug walked his daughter up the stairs and to her room. He walked back downstairs and got a pad of paper out of his desk. On the pad he wrote everything down that he knew about the case. He tried to use branches to see if anything would connect together. It dawn on him that Amy was the last one to see Chad alive and so was the mayor. Doug only needed to ask his daughter one more question in the morning to see if his idea about what happen. He put the pad of paper away and finish his dinner then he went off to bed. A good night sleep is what he needed to clear his mind.

Todd was trying to make Chris feel at home but it seemed the he tried the less it was working. Chris was so upset and in shock that nothing would ever make him feel happy. Todd couldn't believe that this little town already had two murders less then twenty-four hours. On top of that Chris lost his whole family to some crazy person. Todd just hoped when Chris got to a foster care he would have a good experience. Todd put Chris in the guest bedroom and told him good night, he pulled the door around and headed down the hall to his bedroom. It was one hell of a day for him because he never thought he would have to deal with dead bodies like this with some killer. Todd laid in his bed and looked up at the ceiling lost in thought, wondering why someone to all that trouble to make it looked like Ray would kill himself. It took him awhile before he fell asleep.

The next morning brought more of winter weather. Doug made sure he was up before his daughter went off to school. He was in the kitchen making some coffee. He sat down at the kitchen table and his daughter walked in.

"Hey Sue, I got one question for you if u know, was the fight at the house or at the creek?"

"Amy told me it was at the creek, she said sometimes they go there to be alone together."

Doug shook his head and thanked his daughter. He started to get ready for work and head in to the station. Doug thought that Todd was already there, Beth McQueen was there, she was Doug dispatcher at night. Doug needed to hire some deputies but the mayor said it would have to wait until the first of the year, which was about two in a half months away.

Todd made it to the station late because he had to drop off Chris at school. Todd walked in and gave a good morning to Beth. She was still sleepy from yesterday because she worked a little over to help out. Beth was thirty-six years old, she had long red hair and she loved her job. She like Todd a lot and wanted to date him but they were both shy so she knew that she would have to build up the courage to ask him out. She waved bye to him and told him she would bring him some supper later.

Todd waved back and decided the needed to call a social service worker about Chris. Doug came in shortly after Todd called. "Well the social worker said Chris has to stay with me until January because they don't have a home for him now."

"I guess that will be all right, maybe by then they will have a good home for him," said Doug.

Doug told Todd his news, "Well I found out from my daughter that Amy and Chad had a fight at the creek."

"So you think Amy killed Chad."

"No Todd, I think it might have been the mayor because Amy is small but Tim on the other hand is big enough to overpower Chad."

"Yea, your right, Chad was on the football team and there is no way Amy could be strong enough."

"Now we need to get Amy in here so we could ask her some more questions about anything she might remember about her dad that night," said Doug.

Todd agreed and went to pick up Amy at school. Doug tried to get a hold of the mayor since his daughter was coming in but there was no answer. Doug hanged up the phone and decided how he would approach Amy. He didn't want to scare her and he needed answer, so he would try to be as nice as he could to her. About forty-five minutes later Todd and Amy showed up. Doug had her seat by his desk.

"Hi Amy, how are you feeling today?"

"Well sheriff, I am all right, just having nightmares."

"I am sorry to hear that, I just have a few more questions for you."

"Is it more questions about Chad's murder?"

"It is a little more than that, I need you to tell me what happen that night you both were at the creek."

Amy looked away upset, she knew she shouldn't have told Sue. She all so knew it wasn't her fault because she should have went to the sheriff and told him what happen. She replied, "I will tell you but remember I didn't kill him I loved him.

"I understand but you need to tell me the whole truth."

Todd sat at his own desk writing everything down so they could go back through it. He didn't' want to miss a thing she said it was all important to him. There could be some clue in her story that might tell them who the killer was or who it might be.

"Well Chad was at my house like I said before, when he left he told me to meet him by the creek. I agreed and waited for my dad to fall asleep so I could sneak out. I got to the creek Chad was already there waiting for me. We started to make out but I wanted to talk. Chad of course didn't want that but I kept telling him no, I finally slapped him across his face. He got mad at me and slapped me back causing my nose to bleed. I got blood all over his pants which made him madder. I got scared and told him I would see him tomorrow and I left."

"You didn't stay long after the fight?"

"No sheriff, he tried to say he was sorry but I was to upset and just wanted to leave."

"Did he give you his jacket?"

"No, he wouldn't give that to anyone that was his pride and joy."

"The reason I asked is because he didn't have any pants on and he didn't have a jacket."

"Sheriff he had all those when I left him because I had my own jacket."

"It looked like someone was removing evidence or someone was trying to protect you."

The front door of the station made a loud crashing sound as the mayor came bursting in, "What is the meeting of this?"

"I had to ask her some more questions and I tried to get a hold of you but I guess news travels faster through gossip," said Doug.

The mayor cooled down a little but kept a finger pointed at Doug. He grabbed his daughter but Doug stopped him, "Mayor in need to ask Amy one more question."

The mayor turned bright red and let Doug ask his question, "Amy was your dad home when you got back from the creek that night?"

"I don't remember seeing him I was so upset that I went straight to bed."

"Thank-you and if you think of anything else you give me a call."

The mayor and his daughter left the station without looking back. Doug was worried about Amy because she didn't tell her father about sneaking out that night. Doug walked over to Todd's desk to look at his notes and he knew if they could find the jacket or the pants they would have their killer.

All most two months went by and Doug still did not find the killer. The cold weather was here and it started to snow. Christmas was like a day away and the first of the year was approaching fast. He finally get the extra help he needed. The lead on the mayor turned out to be a dead end. He did know that Ray was murdered and it was not a suicide. If only he could find that jacket he could solve this case. He was getting a lot of pressure from the mayor and accusing him of murder didn't make it any better.

Todd kept to himself and tried to hang out with Chris but with the holidays approaching he didn't talk much. Todd tried to cheer him up but it wasn't working, so Todd let him be. Todd was invited to Doug's for Christmas dinner so he thought that might help Chris.

It was Christmas Eve and the Baker house was filled with Christmas cheer. Doug tried his best but nothing was working for him but as long as his family seemed cheerful that is all that mattered. He let his kids get an early Christmas gift. He was hoping the sweatshirt he got Todd was the right one. No one in the house ever talked about the killings or mention Chad's name because they knew Doug was taking it so hard that he couldn't solve this case. The twins tried to befriend Chris but he didn't want anything to do with them. Doug was in thought and decided to go get Todd and Chris a day early to cheer up Chris.

Todd was on his way home from the store. He got a Christmas card for Chris. He couldn't wait until tomorrow to go to Doug's, maybe they could cheer him up. He pulled in the driveway and noticed the lights upstairs were on, so he knew Chris was home. Todd got out of his car and hurried up to the front door, it was bitter cold and windy. The front door already had some snow on it. He opened the door and made his way to the kitchen. He wanted to make a special dinner for Chris. He grabbed the card and headed upstairs to give it to Chris. He went down the hall and knocked on Chris's door. There was no reply so he knocked again, he didn't hear an answer so he tried the door knob. The door slowly opened to reveal the room inside. He stepped in and was going to put the card on the bed when he notice a dark blue sleeve sticking out from under the bed. He bent down and dragged it out and held the jacket in front of him. He scanned the jacket and saw Chad's name on it. He turned white and doubt started to creep in. He realized that Chris killed his brother and father. He never heard Chris come up behind him with a knife. Chris drove the knife in the center of Todd's back. Todd cried out in pain and fell to his knees. Chris helped Todd up on his feet and through him out the bedroom window back in to the bitter cold.

Doug pulled in to Todd's driveway to see someone flying out of a second story window. Doug stopped the car before he was all the way in the driveway. Doug hopped out and ran over to the body to get a closer looked. He saw it was Todd and a knife was buried in to his back. He went back to his car to call an ambulance. He proceeded to the house, opened the front door and walked up the stairs. He reached the top and continued down the hall and saw a door opened. He already had his gun drawn and peeked inside the room and saw Chris standing in front of the window.

"Freezes right there, do not move."

"I am unarmed and I will not move."

"Why did you do this Chris, why did you try to kill Todd?"

"It is because he found Chad's jacket and my secret was out."

"Why on earth would you kill your brother and father?"

"I didn't mean to kill Chad I was fighting with him because I was mad that he hit Amy."

"So you stabbed him and took his jacket and pants?"

"No, it wasn't like that I always walked home by the creek and happen to see Chad and Amy fighting, so when he hit her and she left I tried to talk to him. He was so mad that he excused me of spying."

"I guess you two fought and you just happen to stabbed him?" asked Doug being very annoyed.

"Well, he got the better of me and hit me and some of my blood landed on his jacket and his pants just like Amy's did. I got so mad and didn't think I took my knife and stabbed him in the heart," said Chris with no emotion.

"Okay, so you took the clothes so you could get away with murder."

"It wasn't like that but I didn't want to spend my life in prison and as for my father he caught me burning the pants in the backyard. He threatened to turn me in but I couldn't let that drunk do that to me. I tried to make it look like he killed my brother and decided to kill himself but I couldn't finish in time because you and Todd showed up."

"Why didn't you burned the jacket?"

"I couldn't it was something that I loved and my brother had it instead of me."

"It was easy for you to just kill people right?"

"No, I didn't want to I lose my temper and Chad didn't deserve a girlfriend like Amy and my father was nothing but a drunk. I just killed them and I am not sorry and now I am going to kill you."

Chris came running forward, Doug pulled the trigger shooting him in the leg and then in the arm. The jacket he was holding the whole time fell to the ground next to his head. Doug didn't even know he was holding the jacket until he saw it on the floor. Doug checked his pulse to make sure he was alive, his pulse was weak but he had one. Doug took a deep breath and was glad he didn't have to kill another kid. The ambulance showed up and put Todd in the back, they had to call other one for Chris. Doug knew that he would go to a mental hospital just because Doug thought he was out of his mind and the way he talked about the murders.

The next day Doug went and saw Todd. Todd was all right with some minor nerve damage but he would be okay. Doug told him he would get better and he would see him back at work real soon. The town would never be the same again because of the murders and even Doug couldn't run away from danger no matter how hard he tried, evil was always around the corner waiting for you.

Endless Times

It all began as a dream but when it came to reality, he was not ready for it. Bob Woods always wanted to fight in a war so when World War III started he was all ready to go fight for his country, well at least he thought he was until he started to get home sick. It was weeks later and he was on a boat to the point of no return, well that was what all the men kept saying, Bob could over hear them.

"I hope this isn't as bad as I heard it was," said one of the man.

Another man said, "I heard people are getting shot and their body parts are flying all over the ground."

Bob started to get scared and he didn't know what to do when they would reach their destination. Their boat made it an island and they were all but in different division. They each had their own mission to do but Bob started to get nervous, his hands started to shake, and he wanted to go home.

A fellow officer came up to Bob to try to calm him, "Hey, how are you doing. My name is Jack."

"Hi, my name is Bob. I am glad to meet you and I am a little nervous."

The rest of the day Jack stayed a long side Bob and this made him feel a lot better. He quit worrying about what might happened to him, Jack had changed his life and he was happy to have met him. The commander kept them on their toes and made them run drills for him. They didn't have much training so this made all the man worried about what they were in store for in the war. It was like throwing meat to the wolves but the men were needed to help their country.

The next morning it was cold and dark. The men had to defend the island they were on because it was important to the Americans. The men just got all their equipment around when they heard loud explosions, some even sounded like loud firecrackers. They followed the noise and it led them to a beach on the other side of the island. The other group they were with yesterday, were all dead. Bob seeing all the bodies lying around became angry, he ran to the beach and up the sand dune. The rifle he carried was light weight but it sounded like a cannon going off, as fired at his enemies. The rest of his division followed him, there was 14 of them counting Bob. They rushed their enemy but it was a suicide mission, only six them made it to a dug out were they could take cover. The commander wasn't going out without a fight, he had three of his men go right, the others to go left, and he would cover them. The enemy's bunker was about 20 yards away and they were using a hug gun, blowing anyone away that came close to them. This however was their only chance to defeat their enemy. The enemy was in this bunker and a big rife was pointing out killing anything in its path. The commander charged toward the bunker with a grenade in his hand, the enemy shot him as he tossed the grenade. The shot was fatal to the commander and he fell, laying on the battlefield with his fellow soldiers. The rest of the men came in from both sides like they were told and opened fire. It didn't matter because the commander's grenade did its job and blew up the enemy.

Bob went to the commander and knelt down beside him and listen to what he had to say, "Listen to me soldier, you are now in command."

Bob shook his head he didn't want this, he wanted to say something but he was speechless. The commander was dead now and he had to led, he stood up and saw four men come up to him. One of the man didn't see a land mine and stepped right on it, the explosion was huge sending his body parts flying everywhere. The rest of the men made sure they were real careful now and made their way up to Bob.

"What do we do now?" said Jack.

Bob looked up at him and spoke, "I guess we continue with the mission. I know there is a headquarters on this island somewhere, we just got to find it."

Bob searched the commander and found a map. He saw where the commander made marks on it with giant circles and little notes on the side telling what each circle met. He shed a tear for the commander, he looked at the other two men he didn't know and told them his name. Their names were Doug and Billy. Jack introduce himself and they were on their way. Bob hoped he would lead them safely to the headquarters, he all so put Jack second in command just in case he didn't make. The best way for them to go was east and stay hidden from the enemy.

A dirt road came in to view as they left the beach. They decided to follow it but stayed in the trees that lined the road. They didn't know how far the headquarters was from them and now with the heat beating down on them they were slowly walking. Bob was sweating so much he had to stop a few times to clean off his forehead and wash out his eye's because the sweat was making them sting. They kept walking but it seemed they were not getting anywhere, the island was huge and the only enemy's they saw were on the beach. He kept wondering to himself, why weren't there more enemies stopping them. He looked up in the sky and saw the setting getting low in the sky. The day was about over and they would have to make camp soon.

The darkness was approaching so they picked a spot to make came. They decided not to have a fire because they didn't want the enemy to spot them. Bob kept listening to the night and the only thing he could hear was an animal catching its prey. A cool breezes was blowing through the air and none of the men said a word about it. To Bob it felt real good after the tremendous heat wave they walked in. Bob had the first watch and it was Jack's turned so he woke him up. Jack stretched his arms, he walked over to a tree and led up against it. There was a rustling sound nearby, Jack heard this and went to go investigate. He leaned forward in some bushes to see if he could see what was making the sound and a pair of hands grabbed him.

In the morning, as the sun roses up, there was nothing but silence. Bob was first to wake up and he thought this was a little weird since a war was going on. He saw the other two men still sleeping and realizes that he didn't see Jack. He hurried to wake up Doug and Billy to see if they saw Jack or relieved him of his post during the night. They both answered no and this made Bob real worried. He walked around the campsite to see if he would noticed anything out of ordinary. He did noticed some broken branches and what looked like someone was being dragged. He motioned for the other two to see what he was looking at and they agreed with him. They hurried to get all their things together and followed the trail.

As they got further in the jungle Bob noticed that all the trees were not the same. A few of the trees he recognize from his hometown, he figured all the trees should be the same on an island. He was lost in thought when they came to a clearing, the sun was so bright it blinded them for a few minutes until their eyes could adjust. They saw what looked like a small town, with buildings and even a town square. The town square was directly in the middle of town, in the center of the square was a fountain. In the fountain was a stone angel looking to the heavens. The war took its toll on this town, most of the buildings were falling apart and there was rumble everywhere. Bob led the way but they slowly took their time to make sure they didn't step on any mines. They made their way to the fountain, Bob noticed a small pavilion next to the fountain, he was positive was not there when they first looked at the town but he couldn't be sure since the fountain could have hidden it. He slowly walked up to it and noticed Jack's water can sitting next to one of the poles of the pavilion. He went to take a closer look and notice a power box on the pole. He slowly opened the power box and saw a button, he pushed the button. The pavilion shook a little, the bench that was in the pavilion roses and revealed a door. He moved forward, motioning for his men to follow him, he could feel his heart pounding in his chest. As they entered the door he realizes it was a long tunnel, the tunnel was lit by lights hanging on both sides of the tunnel, they made their way further in and the door behind them closed sealing them in the tunnel. There was only one place to go now and that was forward. The tunnel was narrow and damp. A musty smell filled their noses and made them feel sick to their stomachs. They came up to a door, which was thick and appeared to be solid. It took all three of them bunch together like sardines to push on the door to get it to opened. The door opened a bunch of lights

"I got him, before he got me," said Billy choking on his own blood.

"You did real well, he is definitely dead, nice shot."

Billy smiled, his eye's closed and he drifted away. Bob said a prayer for him and he was thankful he met him. A hideous laughter came from behind him, he turned around, still kneeling down to see a man standing in a white coat, with jet black hair sticking up, a round face with no facial hair and short with a belly.

"Well, you are the only person to get this far," said the man.

"Who are you?"

"I am Dr. Car, you are in the middle of my project, which I call Project A."

Bob didn't know what to say to that, his brain hurt and he just wanted to get out of this nightmare. All of his men were dead now and he felt like he didn't have long to live either, he didn't want to know about any project. He didn't want to be any ones guinea pig, he wanted to say something to this doctor but he didn't know what he could possible say to a mad man.

"You look confuse, I will tell you what I do. I take a soldiers that have dead and give them life again so they can fight in the war."

Bob finally found his voice and replied, "You make the dead come to life again, like in Frankenstein, are you crazy?"

The doctor walked up to Bob slapping him as hard as he could, "Don't you ever call me crazy. To answer to your question yes I do but this one here was a live human being and he worked out pretty good."

Bob shook his head, the headquarters was a lie and the map telling them to come here was all so a lie. He was all alone now, no one would be coming to rescue him and he was some experiment for the government. The doctor's word started to sink in, he became mad and stood up. He made his way to the doctor, he wanted to get close enough because he had a knife located in his pocket. It wasn't a big knife but it would do the trick, he was about a foot away when the lights came back on. He noticed two soldiers entering the room behind the doctor with weapons aiming at him. He didn't care he would die killing the doctor, he slowly reached in his pocket to get the knife. A hand was placed on his shoulder, this made him turned around to see Jack staring back at him. In one quick motion he took the knife stabbing Jack in the neck. Jack's rolled to the back of his head and he stumbled backwards falling over Billy's dead body. Bob turned back toward the doctor with the blood soak knife, it was too late the two soldiers opened fire on him hitting his chest. Bob fell to the floor covered in blood, he was staring at the ceiling, slowly his eye's closed and darkness consumed him.

Days went by before Bob opened his eyes for first time since he was shot. He was lying in a bed, in a room with bright lights, the walls were white and there was a big mirror in the room. The lights were so bright he was squinting looking around the room, he turned to his right and noticed wires in his arm. He all so had wires in his chest and he could see the scars from where the bullets hit him. He tried to move but his body wouldn't let him, he was still in pain. His head was the only part of his body that didn't hurt when he moved it. He saw a door which was all so white like the walls, the only reason he could tell it was the door because it had a door knob. He felt sleepy but he didn't want to sleep, he wanted to get out. He kept trying to move enough thou it hurt, the door slowly opened and in walked Dr. Car. Dr. Car didn't say anything to Bob just walked over to his I.V. bag and with a needle put some green solution in to the wires that were connected to his arm. The doctor next checked the computer that was hooked to Bob to make sure everything else was okay, as soon as he was satisfied he left the room. Bob eye's wouldn't keep open and he drifted back to sleep.

The next day Bob felt like he had a power boost go through his body. He sat straight up screaming in pain, pulling the wires from his arm and chest. His chest was covered in red sores from the wires he didn't care, he stood up with wobbly legs but he used the bed for support. The door was about ten feet away and he was going to try with all his might to escape. He was about to walk when the door open sending in fresh cool air to his face.

"Well, look who is up and ready for more medicine, ", said Dr. Car.

"I… I don't want anymore. I just want to leave and go back home."

"I don't think you can go home, not anymore since you guy's failed your mission. It is now all over."

"What do you mean over?" said Bob with a frighten voice.

"I guess the war ended in a draw. I still however get to make my creations for the government, besides, they like you."

"The government is going to let you kill innocent people, don't they care about people and what do you mean they liked me?"

"I gave you my solution but it did something different with you. It not only brought you back to life but it made you a super soldier. It gave you strength to heal faster and you can't die. I have your last treatment right here in my hand."

Dr. Car moved toward Bob sticking the needle this time in to Bob's neck. Bob tried to take a step back but it was all ready to late. He became angry because he fought for a government that let him become some ones guinea pig. He saw that the doctor was motioning to the far wall where the mirror was located. Bob could see his reflection in the mirror, he saw that his eyes were bright red, his arms were getting stronger and his whole body felt hot as all his muscles continued to work. He could tell that his rage was helping him, he thought of his family that he would never see again. He kept staring at the mirror, his reflection disappeared and he saw who was behind the glass staring back at him, it was his family. He lost control of his emotions grabbing the doctor by his arm, the strength he had he crushed the doctor's arm. He saw other soldiers standing next to his wife and two kids. He ran at the soldiers killing them instantly. He picked up his wife, his two kids and ran with them up a tunnel.

Dr. Car was trying to get himself up with his one good arm. He needed to escape this island, he knew it was a bad idea for Bob's family to be here but the government wanted to have faster result. He knew rage was the trigger but how fast Bob got there shocked him. He left the white room and made his way up the tunnel, it was only about fifteen minutes since Bob went up the same tunnel. Dr. Car was hurrying but keeping an eye open for any sign of Bob. He made it all the way to the dock on the far side of the town but all the boats were destroyed. He saw body parts all over the dock, he got scared turned to run but a huge needle stabbed him in the neck. He fell to his knees looking up at Bob. The doctor started to scream but his scream were cut short as Bob ripped off his head tossing it in the water. Bob looked at his family, they were waiting for him by the trees, he walked towards them, as he did he was hoping they could start a new life together even thou he was a freak.

Blackness

It was a super hot day in June, where all you wanted to do was sit in front of a fan. Kyle Mason was only 17 and he couldn't wait for school to start in September. He had one more year, then he could get out of this town and go to college. His friends were all on some summer vacation with their family's or to some summer camp being a counselor. His parent's didn't have the money for camp or even take a trip together, they hardly did anything as a family. Kyle had to spend his summer in the heat by finding something fun to do, he did however have his girlfriend Cindy Carmine who lived down the block. She was only here for a while before her parent's shipped her off to her grandma's for the summer. He decided to go see Cindy, he put on his sandals and a muscle shirt. He headed out, even thou it was only a block the sun was so hot all he did was sweat with every step he took. He got to her house, walked up to the porch in the shade which helped out a lot. He felt like he won the lotto because he felt a little cooler in the shade. He knocked on the front door a few times and Mr. Carmine answered the door. Mr. Carmine was a big man with long hair and a beard that he never took care off. Mr. Carmine really didn't like Kyle but he let him see his daughter because he did think they were cute together.

Kyle spoke in a low tone, "Is Cindy here, Mr. Carmine?"

Mr. Carmine nodded his head, turned around and yelled at the top of his lungs, "Cindy get down here, your boyfriend is here to see you"

Kyle never heard Mr. Carmine yell before, it sent cold shivers down his spine. Cindy came running down the stairs with a big smile on her face. She was tall, thin, with blonde hair, blue eyes and 18 years old. She was a year older then Kyle but that didn't matter because they did have a lot in common. Kyle was no fat boy either, he was tall, muscular, with sandy brown hair, brown eyes and he was thin but not as thin as Cindy. She went right up to him giving him a hug, he kissed her on the cheek and held real tight. They both sat on the porch and talked about different things.

Kyle spoke in a serious matter, "When are you going to your grandma's?"

Cindy turned her head away before she answered, "I am leaving tomorrow, I really don't want to go. I'd rather spend the summer with you since this is our last summer together. We only have one school year left and we are both leaving for college."

Kyle couldn't agree more with her, he loved the idea of them spending the whole summer together. He asked her if she wanted to go for a walk and spend the rest of the day with him, since he was leaving tomorrow. She said yes and they started to walk down the sidewalk holding hands in to town. The town wasn't that big about 1200 people lived here, the town's name was Little Valley. Everybody knew each other that is what made this town so great. The business were located in the center of town, while everyone else lived around them. To the north of town was a gravel pit, this is where all the kids would go swimming and have fun.

In the woods near the gravel pit there lived an old man people called Louis. He lived in a cabin with no telephone or any kind of electricity, he lived by himself and he always felt a lone. He was out in his garden checking his vegetables making sure of the kids trampled through his garden. His garden was all he had and he took pride in making sure it was the best. He was a simple man now, he kept to himself and hardly went in to town unless he had to get something important. He was getting in age now and he knew to have a family of his own was well past now. He decided to pull some weeds since he was already in the garden. He slowly got on his knees and started to pull at the weeds. He took a glance up at the sky and he saw that it was getting really dark. He stood up and made his way to his cabin. He found one his lanterns to light, he then thought to himself why it was getting so dark so early in the day. There was a knock on his door, he slowly walked to the door and he felt really scared. He turned the doorknob opening the door, there was nothing but darkness on the other side. His eye's tried to adjust to the darkness to see if he could make out anything, he leaned farther out his front door and just when he thought he saw something it was too late, a huge creature grabbed his face with claw like hands pulling him in to the darkness.

Kyle and Cindy made it to town. They decided to stop at a store to get some candy bars, pop and a small bag of chips they could share. They went to sit on the curb to enjoy their snacks. The heat was unbearable, the candy bars they got were already melting inside the wrappers. Kyle tried to hurry up to eat his, but his fingers got all sticky. He looked up in the sky and noticed dark clouds rolling in towards town. He tapped Cindy on the shoulder to show her the dark clouds.

"Well look at that, I didn't even know it was going to rain today," said Cindy.

Kyle nodded drinking the rest of his pop sweating pouring off his forehead, he then had an idea, "You know we should go to the gravel pit to go swimming, before the rain comes."

"Well that does sound like a good idea, let me go home to get my swim suit on then we can go straight there."

Kyle looked at her and said, "You know you could just where your shorts like me, so we don't waste any more time, just in case the rain starts."

Cindy thought about it for a few minutes, she then agreed with him. They both were headed to the gravel pit and didn't realizes the horrors that lay ahead of them. The walk through the heat was tiring and all Kyle could think about was the cool water of the gravel pit all over his body. The gravel pit was now in sight and the dark clouds still were above the woods. He thought that the clouds were moving pretty slow but with the gravel pit so close he didn't give it another thought. Cindy wanted to race him the rest of the way, so they both took off running toward the gravel pit. They both tied reach the small little beach that was right before the water's edge. They started to walk in the water, the water felt like warm bath water, they were hoping if they went farther out the deep water might be cooler. They got to the deep end, he was the first one to dive in the water, Cindy was about to but slipped on the water's floor making her fall. She got herself and let out a little yell, she was smiling to herself when she thought she heard a scream coming from the woods. She looked for Kyle he was still under the water, she waited for him to surface.

As he came up to the surface she urgently said, "Kyle did you hear someone scream, just a few minutes ago?"

"No I didn't hear anything, I was under water. Do you think you heard someone?"

Cindy didn't answer him, she had a shiver run down her back. They both were just looking at each other, then he swam over to her to hold her hand. He could see how scared she was by her face expression. They both were just swimming in place when they heard other scream this time which sounded like a loud siren. Cindy squeezed Kyle's hand really tight and all the color drained from her face. They realizes the sound was coming from the woods, he wanted to go investigate because he wanted to make sure old man Louis was all right. She didn't like this idea but she knew Kyle did have a kind heart.

Kyle entered the woods by himself, she was too afraid to go in. The woods was dark and he could hardly see anything, he knew where the cabin was because he was sent there to complete a dare that his friends sent him on. He kept his hands out in front of him so he wouldn't ride in to trees or trip over anything. He could just make the outline of the cabin through the dark. He was scared to shout out for the old man, instead he just listen to see if he could hear any noises. The whole woods was silence, except the sound of his feet crunching on broken branches. He made his way to the front door of the cabin, he felt around for the doorknob slowly turning in. He opened the door, the inside of the cabin was darker compared to the outside. He took a couple of steps in and smelled a musty smell. He tried to hold his nose but it was too late, the smell was to strong. He kept running in to things and stepping on stuff. He was trying to get his eye's to focus to the darkness like he did in the woods. He felt around in the air and his hand came across a table. He was feeling on the table with both hands now, his hands came across a box, he shook the box and he could hear something shaking inside. He opened the box a little and smelled sulfur. He knew the box was filled with matches, he decided to light one so he could see through the darkness. He lit the match, he could see now and noticed the cabin was messy. He heard some noises on by his feet, he had to light another match the first one went out burning his fingers. He lit another one lower it to the floor, he noticed all these bugs crawling all over the cabin floor. He dropped the match holding his stomach, he wanted to throw up. He left the cabin walking the back the way he came, the darkness seemed to follow him, he was out of the woods but he didn't see Cindy anywhere. She told him that she would wait at the edge of the woods, he knew that she wouldn't go anywhere by herself because she was scared. He had his hands on his head trying to think, a noise made him turned and old man Louis came running from the woods.

Kyle noticed right away that the old man's eyes were missing, Louis had his mouth opened in terror running right in to Kyle. Kyle didn't know what to do, he just held on to Louis as blood was streaming out of his eye sockets. Kyle wanted to scream but his thoughts were racing and he didn't know what to do.

The first thought in his head was ask about Cindy, "Did you see my girlfriend, Cindy Carmine? She was here waiting for me by the woods."

"I... I didn't see her, but I did hear someone scream. I bet he took her," said Louis in a scared voice.

"Who took her?"

Louis was trying to answer but he started to shake, his lips turned purple and he quit breathing. Kyle kept looking at him, he finally let go of him and watched as he fell to the ground. Tears started to form in his eyes, he didn't know who took Cindy and he didn't hear anyone scream. He had to get some help, he heard some noises from the woods, he looked to see a skeleton like hand on one of the trees. He panicked and started running away, he heard some more noises so he looked behind him to see the body of Louis was gone. He took another quick glance at the woods and he saw red eye's staring back at him from the woods.

Kyle didn't stop running until he reached his house. He thought his parents could help him, there was no sign of them and he started to panic some more. He then thought of Cindy's parents and decided to go to her house to see if they could help him. He ran out the front door and down the block. He had this urged to look behind him, he turned around to see the dark clouds were moving fast. This scared him a little because he knew earlier they were barely moving, when he was at the gravel pit. He turned back around and ran all the way to Cindy's house. He ran up the steps to the porch, he started pounding on the door. Mr. Carmine answered the door and his face showed concern.

"Mr. Carmine, Cindy is lost in the woods," said Kyle losing his breath with every word.

Mr. Carmine slapped Kyle across the face before he could say other word, Mr. Carmine spoke in an angry tone, "You were to keep an eye on her you little brat."

Kyle was shocked that he just got slapped, his parent's never raised a hand to him as far as he knew, he was going to speak but Mr. Carmine said, "Why is there blood all over you?"

Kyle was lost for words, he wanted to answer right away but he just didn't know how. Mr. Carmine mad at getting no answer pushed Kyle out of the way. He hoped in his truck heading toward the gravel pit to find his daughter.

Kyle still standing on the porch saw the truck speed off down the road. Mrs. Carmine came up to Kyle giving him a quick hug.

"I am so sorry my husband lost control and hit you. I know he didn't mean to do it. I overheard you talking to him and I know it's not your fault."

Kyle turned to look at her and noticed a big bruise on her arm. He knew now why Cindy's mom always had bruises. Cindy would just laugh it off and say that her mom was clumsy. He just gave her a smile nodding that he understood, they both watch the truck now what they could see of it driving toward the dark clouds. Kyle realized now that the dark clouds were causing some kind of blackness and Mr. Carmine was driving right in the middle of it.

"Kyle, why don't you come in the house? Cindy will be all right, she will come home by herself or with her dad."

Kyle followed Mrs. Carmine in the house, they both went to the kitchen. Mrs. Carmine poured a big glass of lemonade for Kyle. He took it, thanked her and started drinking it. The cool lemonade felt good on his throat, he didn't realizes his mouth was so dry. Mrs. Carmine offered him a seat at the kitchen table, he accepted and they both sat down. They just stared at each other not saying a word, he however wanted to tell her about the creature he saw but thought better of it. He didn't want her to think he was crazy and he really didn't want to upset her.

Mr. Carmine realized that it was getting darker so he turned on his headlights to see thru the blackness. He was all most to the gravel pit when he saw an outline of a body standing on the side of the road. He brought his truck to a shrieking halt, he immediately got out of his truck grabbing his flashlight from the glove compartment. He shined the flashlight to see if he could see the body that he passed a few minutes ago.

Mr. Carmine heard some noises, he turned around and said, "Cindy, is that you? It's your daddy."

There was silence for a few minutes, then a high pitch scream rang out scaring Mr. Carmine. He wanted to yell Cindy's name again but couldn't find the words, shivers ran down his spine. He started to walk back to the truck and saw Cindy standing by the headlights, a relief came over him and he was so happy to see her. He went to go give her a hug but before he got to her something grabbed him from behind. He turned around to see two red eye's staring at him and before he could say anything razor sharp teeth dug in to his neck. He tried to reach for Cindy to help him but she stayed where she was not even moving to save her father. She gave a little smile that her father couldn't see, she was happy that he was dying, she knew now that he couldn't hurt her anymore or her mother. It really didn't matter anymore what else happen because she knew everyone in town would have to die including her mother. As her father laid on the street his still body bleeding out his life source, the creature and Cindy started walking towards town, as the blackness was covering everything up.

It was two hours later, Kyle and Mrs. Carmine were getting worried because there was no sign of Cindy or her father. The blackness covered the town now and all the power was out. They two of them were still in the kitchen using candles that Mrs. Carmine found in a drawer. They were too scared to go outside because they kept hearing screams and gun shots. At one point Mrs. Carmine did try to go outside but Kyle stopped her, she started to cry and rock herself in the chair. He was pacing now back and forth trying to figure out what to do next. He was lost in his thoughts when he heard someone knock on the front door. They both looked at each other in silence, scared to make a sound. Kyle found the courage to walk to the front door to see who was knocking.

Kyle looked through the peep hole in the door and saw Cindy standing there. He couldn't believe his eye's, he hurried to open the door as he did he saw a neighbor threw the darkness putting an axe in to another neighbor, they were really close to the house. This scared him, he grabbed Cindy pulling her in the house and hurrying to shut the door. He gave Cindy a big hug, crying in to her shoulder, her mother came right over hugging them both and she started crying too.

"Mom, could I have some water please?"

"Of course my dear, be right back."

"What happen to you? I tried to find you but you disappeared."

Cindy smiled at him and gave him another hug. Her mother came back with the water and Cindy took a big long drink. She walked in to the living room and sat down in the lazy boy chair. He felt bad that he questioned her right away because he knew that she must have been through so much, just trying to get back home with all the chaos outside. He walked over to her kneeling beside her next to the chair. Mrs. Carmine just stood in the entry way looking at her daughter with concern.

Cindy took a deep breath, holding her cup of water really tight, "If I tell you what happened, you must believe me. I know it's going to sound strange but it's the truth. I was standing on the edge of the woods waiting for you to come back. I felt something grab me and when I turned around there was this creature with skeleton hands, he had razor sharp claws. The creature's skin was a grayish color and I just stood there not moving."

Cindy started to cry, Kyle put an arm around her to comfort her. Mrs. Carmine started to cry and she hugged her self. She knew her daughter was telling the truth and this scared her. He urged her to continue her story when she felt she was up to doing it.

Cindy nodded and continued, "The creature started talking to him in a raspy voice. It told me that I was chosen because I am an innocent. It then touched my stomach, which made me sick at first then I fell to my knees. It then continued to talk, saying it brings the blackness to consume souls for its offspring and I was the carrier. I really didn't understand what he was saying I was so scared. I then heard my dad yelling for me, my dad saved my life by giving his own so I could run from the creature."

Kyle looked at Cindy with his mouth hanging opened, the words she just spoke were so shocking. He did believe her because he did see the skeleton like hands. He knew that they had to leave town since this creature was responsible for the blackness and the chaos that was going on in the town. He knew that were not safe, he stood up grabbing Cindy's hands so he could help her up. He gave her another hug, holding her tight in his arms.

"We need to leave town. We are not safe here, I think we should try to find some weapons so we can defend ourselves and make it to your mom's car."

"I agree with you Kyle," said Mrs. Carmine.

Cindy didn't say anything but just gave a big smile to the both of them. He made his way to the kitchen to find some weapons but all he could find were some big knives. He took three, giving each one of them a weapon. Mrs. Carmine kept shaking, she was trying to hold the knife steady but she was having no success. He went and found the cars keys to Mrs. Carmine's car. They all lined up at the front door, they had to be real quick to get to the driveway, the blackness will slow them down and he didn't want to run in to any neighbors.

Kyle opened the front door and they all went in one big motion, there was still blackness but a bright moon showed above casting an eerie glow over the street. He knew that wasn't there before when he opened the door for Cindy. He didn't want to think about that now, he just wanted to get to the car. They made it to the car and didn't see any crazy neighbors. He decided that he would drive, Mrs. Carmine sat in the back seat and Cindy took the passenger seat. He started the car and floored it down the driveway, he turned the car going toward his house. He was hoping his parent's might be alive, as he dove the one block they could see bodies lying everywhere. He looked at Cindy to see if she was all right but she had no expression on her face. He could hear Mr. Carmine crying in the back seat but there was not one tear on Cindy's face. He just turned to look at the street in time to see his dad standing there with a bat in his hand. He stomped on the brakes being just inches from his dad. He grabbed his knife that he put in the center console of the car and got out.

"Come here boy, let me give you what I gave your mom," said Mr. Mason

Kyle stood looking at his father and he became so angry. He ran at his father with the knife held high in the air. The knife came down right in top of his father's head and they both fell together on the street. Kyle stood up, looked at his father pulling the knife from his head and repeatedly stabbed him over and over. He was now covered in blood from head to toe. He laughed to himself but he heard a loud scream from down the street. He looked and saw the creature walking towards him in a slow pace. He became full of rage and ran after the creature holding the knife tight in his hand. The creature didn't move or try to run away but it held its ground. Kyle didn't care and started to stab the creature in the midsection, the creature clawed at Kyle's back making him scream in pain, this didn't stop him and he continued to stab the creature. The creature finally fell to the ground dead and Kyle let out a sigh of relief falling to his knees.

The blackness was disappearing and Kyle could see daylight. He never been so happy to see the sun. He heard a scream behind him and turned to look to see Cindy standing before him with her mother's head in her hand. She gave him an evil smile and threw the head at him.

"Why would you kill your own mother?"

Cindy screamed again saying, "You are so dumb. I am the chosen one. My mother was trying to keep me in the car and I couldn't take it anymore, so I had to get her out of my way. You killed the creature that help me understand my true purpose in life, now you must die."

Cindy walked up to him grabbing his neck, he tried to fight her off but he was too weak. She pulled hard, ripping his head clean off his shoulders. His face showed signs of pain but she didn't care for him anymore. She tossed his head aside and made her way back to the car. She sat in the driver seat and saw the rest of her mom's body on the passenger seat, she kicked at the body until it fell from the car on to the street. The car was still running so he put in drive, leaving the town behind her. She knew she had to find a safe place to live, to raise her child of evil.

The Door

The house sat in the best part of town. The neighborhood was friendly. The front yard was pretty with a row of bushes out front. A sidewalk led to the huge front porch with a rocking swing by the front window. The house looked safe and inviting. The people who lived there were the best neighbors you could have. The family that lived there had a young boy named John Saw. He had short dark hair, about five four and was thin.

It was summer and John's birthday was only a couple days away. He was turning thirteen. He didn't have a lot of friends, really he only had one best friend Lisa Fern. She was already thirteen and couldn't wait to come to his party. A lot of boys at the school thought it was funny that John had a girl as a friend. This didn't bother John, she was the only one there when he needed someone. She seen him one day crying and went over. He told her how the other boys made fun of him and pushed him around. She went right over to the bullies and showed them who was boss. Right after that John befriended her. They always hanged out and played together.

Having a small birthday party was just fine with him, as long as Lisa could be there. He didn't feel that he was spoiled because he was an only child. He just felt important. His parents always made a fuss over him no matter what. Both of his parents worked now since he was in school full time. Every night they would sit down for dinner and have a great time. Some days they would play games or just sit around to read a book.

John really loved his family. He stretched his arms over his dark hair, taking in a yawn at the same time. He quickly got dressed and headed downstairs for breakfast. His dad and mom are standing by the counter with coffee mugs in their hands.

"Well, hi, there son."

"Good morning, dad."

"Mom, why do you always make a fuss over me like that?"

"You are growing up and my little boy is disappearing."

"Oh, mom, you know that is not true. I will always be your little boy."

His mother tried to give him another kiss but his time he avoided her. His parents were getting ready for work.

"Son, you will be all right while mom and I are gone."

"Yes, dad, don't worry. I won't answer the door to strangers. I am old enough to take care of myself."

His dad just smiled and rubbed his son's hair. He looked up into his father's eyes and saw how much he loved him. He couldn't wait until he was home alone. He just wanted to see what it was like to have the house to himself. He knew that he would explore the house just to see if he could find any gifts.

It didn't take long for his parents to leave as he was eating his breakfast. He didn't want to look too excited for his parent's to be gone. His parents were long gone before he started his search for his gifts. The house seemed different to him.

The day was going to be warm and sunny. His mom told him to make sure he got exercise in the backyard.

Today he had other plans and maybe if he had time he would go outside. He started with the damp, musty and dark basement.

He opened the basement door and stared down into told darkness. He turned the light on, the little light bulb didn't shine enough. The light cast shadows and it gave him a weird feeling. He slowly walked down the wooden steps. He walked down the stairs, they started to creak. When he reached the bottom of the stairs, he looked around to all the items that stretched across the basement. He really wanted to look but fear wouldn't let his feet move. He thought it over and decided to go back upstairs.

He stood in the kitchen and realized that he was sweating. He thought that looking around on the first level in daylight would be better. He searched and searched but no signs of any gifts. He took a lunch break making himself a sandwich along with a glass of milk.

His mind started to wander and the phone rang, bringing him back to reality. Lisa was on the phone, when he picked it up. She was his best friend. Anytime he talk to her he got this warm feeling inside. He tried to invite her over to help. She just wanted to talk and make sure he was all right. He didn't understand girls and what was on their minds. He told her he was fine and hoped she would come see him someday.

The phone made a loud banging sound and it startled him a little. The house seemed a little scary with only him in it. His next step was to check upstairs in the closets and bedrooms. He knew his parents would hide them up there. He walked slowly up the steps and realize what he was doing. He giggled to himself and started to pick up his pace. The first room he checked was the spare bedroom but he found nothing. His parent's room was next and he came up with the same results. Now it was time to check the closets. There was three of them, the first had towels, the second had winter clothing, and the third had some summer coats, old dresses and a few boxes. He moved the boxes out of the way and saw what looked like a door. He couldn't believe it. He pushed the clothes aside and saw the door handle. He turned the door handle and it was locked. He realize that the door took a skeleton key.

His mind started to race and he wanted to find the key. He wondered around the room. He could ask them when they came home. They might even open the door for him. It had to be important or otherwise they wouldn't have put it in a closet. He put everything back and decided to play some videos games, until his parents came home from work.

John realize that he played video games all day. He shut it off and went downstairs to wait for his parents in the living room. He made sure he turned on every light in the house, so he wouldn't be scared. He couldn't understand why his parents were not home yet. They always came home before dark. He started to get worried and then his mom walked in. She smiled and came over to give her son a hug. Dad came in shortly after that holding a bunch of plastic bags.

"Well son, help me out. Your mom went little crazy at the flea market."

John just laughed a little. He went over to his dad and grabbed a few bags.

"By the way. Why is there a door in the closet upstairs?"

His dad had a weird expression on his face. "You must be mistaking there is no door."

"I saw it. The closet in the hallway by my room."

"Oh, well you just don't worry about it ok. Put those bags in the living room by the couch."

John felt that his dad was hiding something from him. His parents never lied to him before. He walked in the living room and notice that his mom also had a strange look.

"I am going to bed now ok."

"Ok son, just don't worry about that door," said his dad.

John hurried up to his room without looking back. His parents scared him a little. As he lay down he couldn't get the door out of his mind. He had to see what was behind it. Even if he had to do it without his parent's permission. He was restless, kept tossing, turning and finally buried his head in the pillow.

When the sun shined through his window waking him up from his restless sleep. He sat up rubbing his eyes wondering first thing where he could find that key. He slowly made his way downstairs to find his parents already eating breakfast. He saw a plate of food on the table where he usually sits. He slowly made his way to his chair and started to eat.

His dad was the first to speak with him. "Are you ready for your birthday party tomorrow?"

John looked right at his dad and put a fake smile on his face. "Yes, I am hoping I get what I want this year."

His dad giggled a little bit and went back to drinking his coffee. John was waiting for more one on one with his dad but it didn't happen. His dad wasn't the sensitive type. John sat staring at his dad for a few minutes longer but there was no success.

He waited for his parents to leave again, so he could get that door open. His parents took a long time to get ready to leave. He kept pacing the floor waiting for that car to back down the driveway. The car finally was leaving and a thought came to his brain, they never said goodbye to him or asked him if he would be ok alone. He opened the hall closet slowly like some kind of creature would jump out at him. He moved the clothes like he did before and there stood the door.

He thought for a while, thinking where the key might be. His parent's room would be a good place to start, but to him that seemed too easy. He walk down the hall trying not to make a sound. He realize what he was doing and laughed at himself. His parent's room was so bright and clean when you entered it. He wondered how they kept it so clean. He scanned the room first with the naked eye, to see if anything popped out at him. When he came to the dresser he saw a little jewelry chest on top.

He walked across their carpet floor. The carpet was shagged, so it had those long pieces that went between your toes. The little jewelry chest didn't seemed locked. He opened up to reveal music playing really loud. He hurried up and shut it waiting for his heart to slow down just a little. He looked around to make sure no one else heard, even though he knew that he was home alone. He took a deep breath and opened it again. The music was playing some kind of waltz but to John he really didn't pay any attention. He found a key on the bottom buried under some old necklace. He looked the key over several times to see if it would work. He was no expert but he thought somehow he could tell. He gripped the key tight in his hand. He made his way back to the hallway closet.

John didn't realize how long he was standing in front of the hallway closet, before he opened the door. It was like all of a sudden, he was in a trace. When he finally came to his sense's shaking his head a little like he had cobwebs in it. He gripped the key so tight that it left indentions in his hand. He shook his hand a little to get the feeling to come back. He put the key in the door, turned the key and heard a clicking sound. A smile spread across his face. He turned the door knob next and the door popped opened.

At first the door made a creaking sound but it went away, when he got it fully opened. He entered the door revealing a round room on the other side. This round room had a huge bay window on the left side. This let all the sunshine in to show the purest white walls John had ever seen.

As he kept staring in this room a thought came to him. There was no cobwebs or any creepy crawling insects anywhere. It was like the room has been kept clean for years. John couldn't understand how that was possible. He surely would see his parents clean and they acted like they haven't been in here at all. In the center of this round room stood a spiral staircase going up. John's thoughts went away from his parents to this spiral staircase. He always wanted to try one, he really didn't know why. He walked to the spiral staircase gazing up. The spiral staircase went up to the ceiling into a hole. He tried to see what was there but it was too dark from where he stood. He grabbed the railing and shook it. The spiral staircase barely moved, to him this was a good sign.

He started up the stairs and you could hear his feet clicking under him. The spiral staircase was metal but it wasn't even cold. As he continued to ascend, a thought crossed his mind. I wonder what my parents would do if they caught me. It would be definitely too late to lie but he wondered what trouble he would get into. A smile spread across his face, he never been in trouble before. His parents yelled at him from time to time but he really never got into trouble. As he kept going he tried to think of all the punishments they could give out. He was getting scared as he entered through the hole.

This room was dark, only a skylight showed a thin ray of light. He could tell that this room was larger but in darkness he couldn't tell. He looked around and noticed a switch on his right side. He walked over to the switch and turned it on. Lights started turning on in the room. The walls on both sides had several paintings on them. On the far wall straight ahead there stood an altar. At least to John from where he stood that is what it looked like. He only saw one altar before that is when he went to church with a friend from school a few years ago. His parents had a fit and he wasn't allowed to see that friend anymore. He walked toward the altar and you could barely hear his footsteps on the hardwood floor. As he got closer to the altar, he notice a huge yellow snake wrapped in a coil on the center of the altar. He was scared and just stood frozen in his tracks.

He didn't know what to do next. He wanted to see what else was on the altar but with that snake there was no way he would. He turned to the walls to look at the paintings. The paintings were weird with creature on them, naked people or just darkness with shadows lurking in the distance. He couldn't understand why people would even want them. It would give the wrong impression to your visitors.

He decided that he had seen enough and was going to leave. He turned around and there stood his parents along with Lisa. The smile on his face fell right away. His mind started to race to think of something to say to help him in his time of need. The only thing he said was, "Hi you come home early."

They didn't respond right away but just smiled. His mother came over and hugged him, his father did the same. When they were done Lisa came over and kiss him on his cheek. John didn't know how to act, he thought for sure he would get into trouble. He notice that more people were coming up the spiral staircase behind his parents. He recognizes the neighbors but not others. They were gathering in this room looking at John with smiles. John started to back up, but someone grabbed him from behind and covered his mouth with a cloth. He tried to fight but he wasn't strong enough and his eyes felt heavy so he closes them.

John didn't know how long he was unconscious for, but he woke up to his dad talking to this muscle bound man. He also realize that he was tied to a wooden table. He tried to focus to hear the conversation. What he heard didn't make any sense.

"Why did you give me time to talk to him? You wouldn't have to do what you did," said Mr. Saw.

"You people are all the same. It had to be done to make sure everything follows the plan. You couldn't be sure he would follow along," said the muscle man.

John's father agreed and walked over to his son. "Hello John I am sorry about this but you were chosen."

"Dad what you talking about? I don't understand what you mean? Please help me out of here?" All these questions cause John to start to cry. He just wanted to go back to his room. He wish he never found the door.

"Son, don't worry the prince of darkness will help you. I will make sure you don't have fear or feel hurt ever again. It will just take a few hours to and you will be fine. I promise I won't hurt you, ok."

John thought his father went off the deep end. He couldn't believe what his father was saying. He couldn't believe that his dad was being serious. He always did what was right, now it seemed that it didn't matter anymore.

"Ok son, I have to take some blood from you. This might hurt a little," said Mr. Saw.

The muscle man had the knife and walked over to them with a smile on his face. John's dad held on to John wrist while the muscle man cut the tips of John's fingers. John didn't notice the wooden cup until they started to put the blood into it. The wooden cup was tall and narrow. It looked like someone carved if from a tree in total darkness. It's shaped was off and not even. He couldn't believe he was thinking these things while he was tied to a table. He squinted in pain.

The muscle man took the odd shape cup to the altar. He lay the cup next to the snake that was now slithering around the altar. He bowed toward the altar and came back to John. John's dad never moved from the table, he stood at John's head rubbing his hair. John just cried and wanted this to be over.

"Now my little man, it's your turned," said the muscle man.

"Dad what does he mean? Why are you doing this, are you crazy?"

John's dad slapped him hard making his face turn red. John had never been slapped before. He got angry. His blood started to boil. The muscle man was hovering right over John now chatting something with his arms in the air. John couldn't figure it out what the muscle man was doing but he didn't feel right either. He couldn't control himself and his body started to shake. He felt like his mind was leaving him. He started to realize that he couldn't control his actions. An evil presence was taking him over and he couldn't stop it. He stared up at the ceiling before closing his eyes.

A few minutes later he opened them to reveal that his eyes were red. A wide grin came across his face. He knew what he was doing but he had no power over his actions. He lifted his arms ripping them free. To him now it was like slicing a knife through butter. He got up, stood there staring at the muscle man and his dad. They didn't know what to do or how to act. John just kept smiling and slapped them both across the face. They hit the floor with a big thud. John just laughed and walked over to the altar. He stood there petty the snake with firm strokes. The snake slithered up his arm and around his neck.

John turned toward his audience of believers and said. "Welcome your prince, you all need to get on your knees and pray for your souls."

In one quick motion they all fell to their knees. John just laughed and it echoed throughout the room. The muscle man crawled over to John's feet asking him to forgive him. John just put a foot on the man's shoulder and pushed him off.

John then grabbed a hold of his dirty shirt ripping it from his body. He again slapped him across the face. The muscle man's face smacked the hardwood floor. John's dad was on his knees in total shock. John walked over to him and told him to rise.

Mr. Saw wouldn't look into his son's eyes but stared at his feet. John just laughed and put a hand on his dad shoulder.

"Why don't you look at me? Are you ashamed of what you created?"

Mr. Saw didn't know what to say or do. He just kept staring at John's feet. It was like his voice quit working and he wanted to tell John how he felt. He was sorry for all the bad things he had done to him. It was just not there it's like it didn't matter what he said, John wouldn't listen. John kept his hand on his father's shoulder squeezing real hard, Mr. Saw cried out in pain.

"See, even my own father fears me. You should all be grateful that I don't make you people suffer."

Most of the people in the crowd shook in fear, others just cried and bowed their heads thinking that today was their judgment day. John found his next victim it was the muscle man. He laughed so loud that the muscle man ears hurt. John dragged him over to the altar where the knife lay. He picked it up and slide it across the muscle man's throat. Blood flowing every all over John. He looked at the crowd not one person made a sound. He saw Lisa with her beauty standing a few feet away. He pulled her close grabbing the back of her head placing a hard kiss on her lips. Lisa smiled not even scared of him, John liked this and pulled her to him even closer. He made sure that she wouldn't get hurt for what he was about to do. He raised his free arm in the air and started to make the people burst in to flames. His mother tried to stop him but he had no remorse for her and burned her too. The room was like one big inferno except for where Lisa and he stood. John's dad never moved from his spot except to grab the knife and take his own life. John walked with ease as him and Lisa walked back down the stairs. He knew he would never come back to this house. He had his own plans now and that included to destroy the world. The sky now was turning black and grey color from the house burning to the ground. Nightfall was coming soon and it would suck them in total blackness.

Printed in the United States
By Bookmasters